JANE LESTER

THE GOLDEN BUTTERFLY

Complete and Unabridged

LINFORD
Leicester

First published in Great Britain in 1976

First Linford Edition
published 2019

A catalogue record for this book is available
from the British Library.

ISBN 978–1–4448–4227–2

Published by
F. A. Thorpe (Publishing)
Anstey, Leicestershire

Set by Words & Graphics Ltd.
Anstey, Leicestershire
Printed and bound in Great Britain by
T. J. International Ltd., Padstow, Cornwall

This book is printed on acid-free paper

THE GOLDEN BUTTERFLY

When Eileen Amberley's longtime friend Richard takes up a position as a doctor at Vickersands Hospital, she goes there herself, to train as a nurse and hope their relationship will lead to marriage. Instead, she finds herself watching the dazzling Heather Maple capture Richard's affections, and is heartbroken. Then she meets the attractive, enigmatic Jeff Watt, who works on the waterfront — and keeps a secret. By the time Eileen discovers the truth, is it too late for the two of them to acknowledge their feelings and make a life together?

Books by Jane Lester
in the Linford Romance Library:

SISTER MARCH'S SECRET
LOVE'S GOLDEN TOUCH
NURSE IN THE EAST
LEGACY FOR LORNA
ROMANCE AT REDWAYS
DR. BRENT'S BROKEN JOURNEY
MATRON'S NIECE
A GIFT FOR DR. GASKIN
WYNDHAM'S WIFE
THE IRISH DOCTOR
THE HOUSE AT CHELTENWOOD

1

I don't think I'll ever forget that train journey, when I first met Heather Maple. It was a golden day in late summer and Richard and I were returning to our hospital. Richard was a houseman now, and I had got through my first year as a student nurse with a little more than success. Some student nurses scrape through, some are moderate, but some — Sister Tutor called them the Chosen Few — had a little something extra. A little something extra that made her have that gleam in her eye, and she sometimes started to talk about the number of Gold Medallists who had passed through her hands. The way she had looked at me before I went on my summer leave, had made me experience a queer little thrill. All I wanted in life was to be a specially good nurse, and to marry Richard Barclay.

Gran said, just before I left her cottage in deep country where I had been restlessly taking my summer holiday, 'You want too much, girl! Best be modest in your ambitions — especially you! With you, it shows. That face of yours is a dead give-away!'

Well, that was all I needed. She had already reminded me that I had better be prepared for the pretty girls to set their caps at Richard. He and I had grown up together. 'Don't consider him your property, just because you were next-door neighbours all your young days!' Gran warned. Gran was an expert at warning, but I didn't mind, because she was something of an expert on the subject. She'd been engaged five times, married three times, and I hadn't even had a 'steady'. But today I was going back to Vickersands General and District Hospital and I had Richard with me. I literally walked on air.

We talked 'shop' for the first hour. With our usual exuberance we had, during our holiday, cycled around the countryside, and Richard and I had been 'in' on three road accidents, two factory accidents, two 'incidents' on farms near us, and Richard had chalked up two confinements, while his father, the local G.P. had been elsewhere engaged. Gran said we were too ghoulish for words. We discussed them avidly. Richard had a notebook and was working out the percentage of accidents as against illnesses in our district, but all I could think of was that at twenty-four he had his first grey hair, shining at the back of his dark rather short hair, and that he had lots of laughter lines round those blue eyes of his.

The carriage became crowded. In the ordinary way he would have driven me home and back to the hospital but he had lent his old car to someone, who had bashed one wing so he had left it to be repaired. He didn't mind the carriage being crowded. Richard's temperament was as easy as his ready smile. He adored people in the mass. I don't think he had ever shown any particular preference for one person more than another: he just loved them all.

And then Heather Maple had got in. I didn't know that was her name then. She was a thin girl, not too tall, with the sort of look on her face that suggests that life has given her a rotten time but that she isn't going to let it beat her. Richard jumped up and helped her in with her luggage. It was plentiful, heavy, rather shabby, and her clothes were odd, as if she had gathered them from all over the place, regardless of their newness or particular fashion, but for the sake of having a full outfit to put on. Yet, on her, they didn't look peculiar. She wore them like a banner, I found myself thinking, helplessly. Any other girl would have been ashamed to look — so — well — *different*, but not her.

Richard started to stow her luggage away for her. One piece was a cardboard box tied up with string, and a sleeve of a frock was peeping out. Richard dropped it, and other people were pushing through, and all was confusion and he went red, a thing I've never seen him do before. But we were finally settled and the train started off again, and we returned to our note-taking. But it wasn't the same. We were conscious of that girl staring at us.

She had quite vivid eyes: hazel, with long, long dark lashes that simply weren't false. And her hair, so black, and so elaborately curled that I was sure it must be a fantastic wig, seemed to attract Richard's eyes, too, because in the end he gave up trying to do these statistics of ours, and then somehow Heather Maple was in the conversation, and we were all three talking, and then it was only Richard and Heather.

She had a husky voice, and the sort of mouth that reminds you of a child's, with an oddly innocent look about it that I at once distrusted. I've seen too many girls come through Casualty at night with a mouth that shape. And yet she fascinated me.

She said, 'I daresay I shall find something.' I didn't know it then, but that was her philosophy in life, and for her, it worked.

Richard said, 'But I say, do you mean to say you don't know where you're going to stay in Jedminster . . . '

'Well, no, I booked there because that was the amount of money I had left. It just took me as far as there.'

'But what will you do for food? And you must find digs or something,' Richard protested.

'Perhaps I'll busk a little,' she said gently, and she smiled, and Richard couldn't stop looking at her. Well, neither could I, come to that, and try as I would, I couldn't dislike her. That smile was so winning, and she was so pretty. She explained, 'It sounds awful, doesn't it, but it's the way a lot of people get noticed and go on the stage, you know, and that's what I really want.'

Richard looked helplessly at me. I heard him say, 'What can we do about this, Eileen?' and then he was introducing me to her, and introducing himself, and she said she was fascinated that such a young man could possibly be a doctor.

I could cheerfully have kicked her, but the feeling didn't last long, because she went on, 'I have had experience of doctors and hospitals. My family were all killed in an accident. A bus colliding with a lorry. I was injured too, but not much. I haven't got anyone now, but I know a lot about hospitals and doctors.'

Her father, she said, had been an artist, and her mother just couldn't leave a piano alone, and then finally had had to give piano lessons to help out when so many children came along. Heather had no inhibitions about talking of her family. She had got over the grief stage, it appeared. 'I've been living with an aunt for two years but now she's married again and her husband . . . '

' . . . didn't like you?' Richard said hotly. He obviously couldn't see how any man could help liking Heather.

She blinked a little and glanced at me. Obviously she would have liked to agree with Richard, but perhaps my own expression warned her off that line, for she said simply, 'Actually he liked me too much.' She said it candidly. 'At least, my aunt thought so. Well, they were newly married. Can't say I blamed her,' and even I couldn't feel too nasty towards her after that.

The rest of the journey was taken up with both Richard and me telling her what life at the hospital was like. I don't think either of us could see where this was leading us, but in the end Heather said, toying with the silver paper off the bar of chocolate I'd given her, 'I know nurses live in, and I thought I ought perhaps to get a live-in job, and it seems sensible, I suppose, since I know about the life and I don't faint at the sight of blood or anything, and I'm too sane to think I could make a living on the stage really, not being actually good at anything in that line. I mean, let's face it, a person has got to have something special, to stand a chance, these days. I suppose . . . I just suppose you two couldn't . . . wouldn't really . . . feel like getting me in?'

*   *   *

It was preposterous. Like someone asking if you could get them into a tennis club or something like that, the way she phrased it. But she had this personality about her, which had the effect of making you feel rotten for the thoughts you had about her. I took it up with Richard afterwards, and he admitted that he, too, had felt like that. Heather wouldn't make a nurse; nobody on earth would expect her to. We both agreed on that. Yet we scraped up between us the balance to put to her Jedminster ticket so she went on to Vickersands with us, and Richard saw his uncle, who is in the Path. Lab. who promised to have a word with Matron, who was a friend of his, and I promised to keep an eye on her and see she had some food and somewhere to go till she could get into the Nurses' Home. Well, looking back on it now, it takes my breath away, the things we did on that first day we met her. And all the time I was crying inside with disappointment, because it was to have been my day with Richard. But Gran had known, hadn't she? She had warned me that a pretty girl would snatch him from under my nose, hadn't she? And what did all the years of companionship from early childhood stand for, then, if some stranger could come along and bedazzle a young man as level-headed as Richard?

All very fine to talk, I suppose. I had to collect my bike from Walter Noakes, who had been a patient in my first days on the ward, and who had a special soft spot for me, he always told me. And so I had to be an idiot and tell him about this girl we'd met on the train who had nowhere to go and was so pretty and so gallant that she thought she might have to busk outside the theatre to get enough for a meal, and Wally Noakes was furious to think such a girl had no roof over her head. 'Bring her along to us, nurse! The missus'd love to have her! You know she would, poor little wretch! I don't know, how some parents can — ' and I broke in and said she'd lost all her family in an accident, and that finished it. Wally was almost ready to get out his old banger and go to pick Heather up personally.

Not that that was in any way special treatment. Matron herself (dear motherly Matron who resolutely refuses to be called by the new label) was equally indignant at the thought of such a nice girl not being snapped up to be a nurse. That was after she had interviewed Heather, of course. I can't think what Heather said to her. Heather didn't impress me as being good nursing material, but then Heather did brainwash me into treating her as a young sister, so I suppose it was about the same.

Our hospital was oldish, red brick, and sprawling. Somehow the touch of the modern new system had not reached us. We obstinately went on in the same way and everybody liked it, from the Board down to the patients. The great administrative systems could go for the new filing, the new layout of wards, the new names for the staff, the lot. But not us. We still shivered in our shoes outside the Holy of Holies called Matron's Office, the same as it had always been; and Matron was still terrible in her wrath to the guilty ones, and absolutely a motherish old pet to those who were grieving or homesick. So long as you honestly wanted to nurse, then you were okay.

We still had out-of-bounds things — none of this modern nonsense of pampering nurses because they were hard to get! None of this business of Agency nurses at high prices, which made for bad feelings among the lower-paid staff. No, there were too many girls who wanted to learn the hard way at Vickersands. I don't know why. It may have been the fashion locally. I only know I loved the place come rain or shine, but then I had always walked on air because Richard was on the staff. We had our favourite porters, and we did things for the patients in our free time; we flirted with the younger ones on the medical and surgical staff, we wouldn't have dreamed of flirting with any male patient, and we all, without exception, were terrified of Richard's terrible uncle, who was called Sir Russington Barclay — in a hushed whisper. I think even Richard was scared of him. But apart from that, and the fact that we all approached the Path. Lab. in fear and trembling, there were times when I hated the great man for having thrown in his weight to get Heather into the Nurses' Home.

But only sometimes. At other times I was brainwashed by Heather to like her; everyone was brainwashed by Heather to like her, feel sorry for her, give her a helping hand, but only I had the burden of her. I don't know how she managed it, but against my better judgment I found myself accepting the label of 'Heather's friend' and I gradually became responsible for her.

She wasn't like anyone else. 'If she'd only be a pest and have done with it!' I complained to Frances Trepple one day. 'I wouldn't mind then! But she isn't. It's . . . oh, I don't know.'

Frances twinkled at men. 'It wouldn't be because your dear Richard Barclay walks about nowadays as if he's had something hit him right between the eyes, I suppose?'

'No, it wouldn't!' I snapped. Then I thought about it. 'I suppose I wouldn't mind so much if Heather liked him, but she doesn't seem aware of his existence, you know. Well, not specially. I mean — she likes all men who are young and who help her, but she hasn't tried to butt in between us. Honestly, I can't say she has!' But Frances wasn't impressed by that argument.

I was in my second year, and I had a lot of serious study to do, and I really didn't want to be bothered with a new Lamb. Heather had come in behind the others, too, and she had to pull up her work somehow. I didn't realize what was going on at first. One day Richard broke a date with me (not a serious date, but one of our matey walks along the shore) and he didn't tell me why, but I found out later that he had stayed in to hear Heather say her bones. Frances wasn't going to tell me. Another of our year was talking about it and didn't know I was around. She was fed up to think I'd heard her. They weren't mischief-makers; they were my friends. And I didn't think any more about it. The skeleton known as Pete hangs in a cupboard. When we were in our first twelve weeks, we stuck a moustache on him and a wig. It must have given poor old Sister Tut a nasty shock when she opened that door. But we never ever thought of bearding an unsuspecting houseman to hear us say those bones! We stayed in and heard each other.

Another time I was supposed to be going to the shops with Richard to choose a pipe for his father. Dr Barclay had brought me into the world. I suppose I looked on him as a sort of uncle. We always helped each other choose pipes for him, because he went on and off them. It had been a big ugly smelly Meerschaum not so long back. Now, it seemed, he was hankering for a small, very nifty little briar he had seen the relative of a patient smoking. And I wanted to buy him a lovely oak pipe-rack I had seen. It was one of those special afternoons, and I had looked forward to it. Richard sent a belated message that he couldn't go that day; he was tied up. The most miserable junior on our floor, whom nobody liked, made it her business to tell me that Dr Barclay had taken the new nurse with the black frizzy hair out in his car.

'Frizzy' was not a kind word to apply to Heather's hair, which was one mass of corkscrew curls, and later found to be naturally curly, and not a product of a hairdressing salon, as I had at first uncharitably thought, following the conclusion that it wasn't a wild wig. But at that moment I could cheerfully have condoned that hateful little junior for anything she had said about Heather.

Later, Richard put a friendly arm around my shoulders and said, 'You didn't mind, love, did you, but our little friend Heather was so unutterably miserable that I got the bright idea of taking her down to the Public Library to look up a book there to help her.'

My Gran had hammered it into my head never to let a man see, if you could help it, that you were mean-spirited about some other female, so I said, 'Oh, well, let's hope it did the trick!' in an unnatural bright voice that Richard should have known was false. But he didn't. He looked fondly at me, squeezed my shoulders and said, 'You are a brick, you know! I knew you'd understand! But then look at the way you look after her! I'm sure you're a lesson to us all!'

Which was what really brought things to a head, I suppose, because next morning — with a new date that afternoon in view for the pipe-choosing fixed with Richard, I found myself confronted by a tearful Heather and a file in her hand. 'You've just got to take it to the Path. Lab. for me, Eileen! I won't go there! I hate Richard's uncle! He's an absolute meanie and he terrifies me! You go! You're . . .' and she searched around in her mind for a descriptive word, but obviously boggled at insulting me with the word 'brave'.

'What am I?' I asked coldly and clearly.

'You're kind and you won't let me be upset by any more of the top brass,' she said quietly and simply. 'I've just got a rocket from someone called Dr Vanman — '

'But he's a nice man!' I protested. 'What did you do?'

'Spilt a patient's orange squash all over him,' she said.

'But you're not supposed to be on the wards yet!'

'Oh, I wasn't. I was carrying it upstairs for a patient who'd been visiting and forgot it, only the top wasn't screwed on, and I skidded on the new polished floor and I wasn't supposed to be there only I was just sneaking in to look for Richard — '

I wished she wouldn't keep calling him Richard and I was infuriated by the expert way in which she got one into a corner, so that one just had to do what she wanted. And now this! Being caught in the hospital proper when you were only a Lamb is still pretty high on the 'sin' lists in most hospitals, but in ours it was practically unheard of. I said, 'But Dr Vanman! If you've upset him, then you really *are* for it!' But my anxiety was really for myself, not for her. Practically speaking, she had somehow got herself put in my charge, just because of the peculiar way in which she insinuated herself into my hospital that day on the train.

She managed to look honestly upset about it. 'I've made your life an absolute mess, haven't I?' she said quietly. Even I didn't want to doubt her sincerity. 'I think I'd better go and tell matron I'll resign. It's the only way,' she said, with a sigh. She looked down at the file in her hands. 'But it's no use, I just haven't got what it takes to deliver this. After all, it was the word of Sir Russington that got me into the hospital, and he'll be more livid than Dr Vanman, when he hears.'

'Well, don't tell him. Just knock on the Path. Lab. door and push it at him and run. I can't go — I haven't time.'

She looked as if she were going to burst into tears. 'Neither have I — ' she shouted. 'And if I'm leaving, I don't see why I should! Besides, Richard's waiting to drive me into Nosterbridge,' and she thrust the file at me and ran.

I had been on my way to my coffee break. I would lose it if I went over to the Path. Lab. Different if I'd been asked to take the thing, but to do it for someone below me, well, it just had to come out of my own time. Which didn't help matters. Out with Richard, indeed!

I simmered about the whole thing all the way over to the Path. Lab. Although I didn't run (which is only allowed for emergency or haemorrhage) I made good speed, and I was almost at the door of that awful place when I skidded to a halt, as realization hit me. If Richard were taking that girl over to Nosterbridge, it would take the rest of the day. He had either forgotten our shopping date or had decided I would 'understand' — a word that was fast becoming overworked and wrongly used, in this present context, I considered.

I knocked smartly (and perhaps a little too loudly) on the door and was answered by the usual growl. The great man had a small room to himself but he was usually at a special place at one end of the laboratory surrounded by the paraphernalia of his pet thing, searching for some bug that nobody had ever found or hoped to. Hunched in darkness, as usual, the pool of strong light catching only the top of his bent head and his strong-framed glasses, he growled something and pointed vaguely at another bench, without looking up. Charming manners, I thought, as I shoved the file down and prepared for flight, I again asked myself why he had bothered himself about a scrap of flotsam like Heather.

I didn't manage to escape, however. He suddenly shouted, 'Who the blazes are you?' and before I could answer, he said, 'I asked for Nurse Maple to bring it!'

His voice echoed eerily in the big place. He had leaned back to see who it was, so now he was in deep shadow, more deep by the contrast of the strong light on his test tubes and papers. I felt it was extremely unfair of him to hide in the shadow like that, and to make matters worse, he had taken off his glasses and was rubbing his eyes. His face was completely covered, but he could obviously see me.

I always get hot-tempered about the Big Shots who lean too hard on the little people who can't answer back. Gran's warned me, time and time again, but I always forget at the heated moment. I snapped back at him, 'Nurse Amberley, sir, second year, and Nurse Maple pushed the file at me and ran off so I had to bring it. I knew it would be wanted urgently.'

He grunted, replaced his glasses and hunched himself over work again. 'Tell her to report to me the minute you see her,' he said. Well, at least, I think that was what he said. It was too muffled to hear clearly, and I'd had enough. I got out of there quickly before he decided he'd have me on the carpet, too.

I marched back to the hospital, absolutely furious with Heather and Richard, and his horrible uncle. That horrible little man, sitting there taking it out of me, and what had I done? And, what was more, what was I intending to do, I asked myself suddenly, for the rest of what was to have been a very happy day, with Richard, to choose a birthday present for his father?

I finished my duty on the wards, had my lunch, put on my positively oldest things — a check shirt and a dark sweater with a polo neck, which turned out to be too warm for the day — and I took myself down to the old end of the town, where the beach was littered with broken small craft from the last storm, and rusty ironwork from a previous attempt to shore up the crumbling cliffs. It was a nice miserable place to go and be miserable in, I told myself.

Which was a pretty silly thing to do on an afternoon off. I should have gone to the pictures or taken a bus ride or something that would have taken my mind off things. Instead of that, I leaned on the same bollard that Richard had sat on last time and that finished me. Hating myself, I took refuge in the hurting tears of anger and humiliation. I knew I had lost Richard, even though he was still friendly with me. I knew that even if Heather left the hospital, his heart would go with her, even though he himself might, on the face of it, go back to the old easy relationship with me. And that was the most hurtful thing of all.

'Is this a private place for bawling, or can anyone join in?' a voice punctured my misery, and I looked up and found the man by my side, who irritated me about once a week.

I scrambled off the bollard and scrubbed at my face, and glared at him. He stood there much as always, hands thrust into the pockets of the dirtiest pair of cords imaginable, cords that had been used, like the hand-knitted sweater, for working in. A big, dark, strong young man in his late twenties or early thirties with a weather-beaten face. I'd seen him rubbing up the brass on a spanking 45-footer with as much love and care as if it was his own. And I didn't want any waterfront man talking to me in that fashion! I said, 'Please yourself!' and began to march away.

But I couldn't see. I was still blinded by tears, and the next thing I knew was that I was flat on my face, my feet entangled in a mess of hawser half buried in the shingle.

I was never so smartly put up on my feet again in my life. He really was a strong young man. He pushed me down on to the flattish top of a half buried rock and said, 'Better get yourself composed before you pick a fight with me!' Which was just the sort of thing to make one want to fight more. Then he finished heaping coals of fire on my head by handing me a clean white handkerchief, not yet shaken out of its fresh ironed folds. I couldn't think how it could keep clean like that in those pockets of his!

'Been kicked out of your job?' he asked, when I'd finished gulping and scrubbing my face. 'Well,' he added reasonably, 'I know you're a nurse at the hospital, don't I? You usually march along here in uniform.'

So I said, 'Well, I haven't been sacked,' and then, remembering the way I had spoken to Sir Russington, I added, truthfully, 'Not yet, that is,' and out of my misery I said, without being able to stop myself, 'and if I am, it won't be my fault, because he's the most beastly unfair man breathing and he'll love getting me kicked out!'

There was an old crate nearby. Heaven knew what the Council thought it was doing, to leave so much stuff about on the beach! But he found nothing to complain about, as he dragged the thing over and sat on it. 'Who are you talking about?' he asked matily.

'Nobody you'd know!' I snapped. 'Sir Russington Barclay, if you must know! The great man himself!'

'What did he do? Hit you?' he asked, with great interest.

'Don't be silly,' I said scathingly. 'No,

he just keeps most unfairly in shadow so nobody can see him, the horrible little man! And he shouts, and he's rude, and just waves a paw to let you know your usefulness is finished. And I hate him.'

He gave Sir Russington his considered opinion, then said surprisingly, 'He's not like that, aboard *Seamaid II.*'

'*Seamaid II*?' I echoed, the truth dawning on me that this trying young man worked for Sir Russington and would probably be my undoing. 'You *know* him?'

'I think I may say that,' he said modestly, grinning cheerfully. '*Seamaid II* is the white yacht you glare at every time you pass the harbour. Why?'

'Why what? Why do I pass the habour or why do I glare? I didn't know I did glare.'

'Yes, you do. Seen you! Often. Say to myself sometimes, 'Jeff,' I say, 'there's a girl who'd kick you for two pins, if she wasn't pleased with you!' You would too, wouldn't you?'

I got up. 'I don't know what you're talking about.'

'I suppose you don't like the idea of Sir Russington owning a yacht like that because you don't like him,' Jeff hazarded, getting up too. 'Feel all right? You don't look too good.'

'I'm all right, thank you,' I said reluctantly, looking at the mess I'd made of his handkerchief, and I said, 'I'd better take this back and wash and iron it for you. Thanks for the loan of it.'

'Yes, you do that,' he encouraged. 'Then I would have an excuse to say a few things to you. Well, I haven't dared, so far.'

I looked scornfully at him. If there was anything that scared that young man, I'd like to be told what it is.

I suppose, as usual, my thoughts showed on my face, earning a snort of laughter from him. 'You're right, there, girl,' he said. 'Not much worries me. Well, why should it? Got my health, haven't I? When you think how many people haven't, that's something to be thankful for. And I've got the sea.'

'And someone else's yacht to drool over,' I said savagely.

He walked beside me. There wasn't much I could do to stop him, and anyway, as I wanted to fight someone, and get it out of my system, I thought it might as well be him.

He looked thoughtfully at me, then offered, 'You're only cross because Sir Russington's nephew Richard hasn't got a yacht.'

It was so true that I felt my face flame up to the hairline, and I was shaking with anger.

I didn't answer. It was nothing to do with him.

He went on, as if I wasn't hopping mad with him, 'Wonder what it's like to have a girl feel like that about you?' He spoke softly, half to himself.

'You should know!' I retorted. I rarely saw him without some girl looking yearningly at him; Elsie from The Rose and Crown, flying across the road, her face all lit up, to speak to him. The girl from the photo kiosk trying to persuade him to go in and have a free picture done. I'd seen him at the newspaper kiosk, being served with yachting magazines for his lord and master, and if the girl behind that counter could have, she'd have made him a present of them. And he was pretending he never had women look sloppy over him! Something about him had always enraged me.

Especially now. He just grinned cheerfully at me and said, 'Oh, no, I'm destined to be a confirmed bachelor. Richard, now, he's different.'

'Why don't you call him Dr Barclay?' I said fiercely.

He looked surprised, then those dark grey eyes of his twinkled at me and he said, 'Oh, is he qualified now? Then Dr Barclay it is,' and he kept staring at me, because I'd coloured again. One of the things that angered me was that people tended to treat Richard as if he was still a medical student. It was because he looked so fresh and clean and youthful and cheerful, and not like the hard-bitten doctors who peopled the hospital, running a losing race against time and the constant stream of sick and injured who entered our doors.

'I suppose you wouldn't like to come aboard the *Seamaid II*?' my companion said suddenly. 'I take it you know something about sail craft?'

'You must be mad!' I exploded. 'I wouldn't come aboard Sir Russington's yacht, not for all the gold in Egypt!'

'Well, I know when he wouldn't be there,' he said reasonably.

'That's not honest!' I stormed. 'Besides, it'd be my bad luck to have him alter his mind and come aboard and catch me. I have awful bad luck!' And to my shame I found myself telling him about the coming of Heather, and the way she had insinuated herself in my life and ruined everything, and I laid it all at Sir Russington's door for persuading Matron to take her.

'Did he do that?' Jeff asked, with real interest.

'Oh, is there something about your employer that you don't know?' I jeered, and now it was his turn to colour.

'And you say you've never even seen him face to face?' he asked thoughtfully.

'Well, what about it? It's not my fault that that nasty little man hunches over his test tubes and doesn't have the decency to let the full light fall on his face, is it?'

He looked down from his great height at me. Well, he was a good six inches taller than I was, which gave him a horrible advantage, and his breadth and strength made me feel very weak and frail, the sort of girl who couldn't be trusted to walk on a beach without bawling, or getting mixed up and falling over half-submerged rubbish like this morning. And he said, 'You shouldn't judge a chap till you've seen him, you know. After all, there might be reasons for him recommending that girl, things like doing anything to get rid of tiresome people bothering him when he wanted a bit of peace and quiet. Have you thought of that?'

2

I was very much intrigued about Sir Russington now. He really couldn't be such an awful little man, could he, to keep an employee like Jeff so loyal and ready to make excuses for him?

I determined to ask Richard about his uncle. After all, I should be seeing Richard, with one of his new selections of excuses about letting me down over the shopping spree.

Richard was on duty that night, and I didn't have a chance to talk to him until next day, and then it was when we happened to pass each other crossing the great space outside the front of the hospital. It was all asphalt, with one or two circular flowerbeds let into it. A strip of grass round the very edge gave a welcome bit of colour, in what would otherwise have merely been a barracks — a beloved barracks it was true, but not very cheerful to look at. I always looked at the grass strip, marvelling on how nice it was kept, and in doing that, I almost missed Richard. He would have walked right past me.

I stopped in my tracks and called him sharply. He turned, focused with an effort, then clapped a hand to his forehead. 'Oh, good grief, Eileen! I've just remembered! Yesterday! Dad's pipe! Golly, are you so mad you'll never speak to me again?'

'I thought you weren't intending to speak to me, Richard,' I said, frowning. 'You've never forgotten before, when you said we'd do something.'

'I know, love. How can I show you I'm sorry?' and he seemed upset out of all proportion.

'What about tomorrow?' I asked him. 'Same time, same place?'

Same time, same place. What heart-breaking words they can be! Especially as Richard was looking pink and bothered. I've never seen him look like that before.

'Well, as a matter of fact,' he began, haltingly.

'Good heavens, if you've said you'll take Heather out tomorrow why don't you say so? It's all right!' I said bracingly. 'Then we'd better go today. I daresay I can change duties with Frances. Sister won't care as long as she has a full complement. She's a good old scout.'

'Yes, well, it isn't as easy as that,' he said, looking fussed. 'Heather's going out with young Stanton.'

'David Stanton? Well, that's fine! He's about her type,' I said, managing to smile. Things began to look a little brighter.

'Yes, but the young devil stood her up, and when she asked me if I'd take her tomorrow, and I started to say I couldn't, she looked — well, she went all white and pinched, and honestly, I thought she was going to faint.'

'Perhaps she was,' I said unfeelingly. 'At the thought of two males standing her up. Well, good gracious, Richard, you don't want to go into competition with a second year student, do you?'

Mistake, mistake, I told myself, gritting my teeth. Just the thing Gran warned me not to do. So I made things worse by saying, 'Oh, well, you're a kind old uncle type so you'd better go ahead and take her, or else she'll come and cry on my shoulder.'

'Don't you *like* Heather, Eileen?' he asked incredulously. 'It was you who took her up, that day on the train!'

'Was it?' I asked, in sheer surprise.

'Yes, it must have been,' he said. 'I confess I'd forgotten it but Heather reminded me of that, and she can't say enough nice things about you.'

Well, I began to see the way Heather worked, after that. And yet — and this puzzled me for a long time — when I ran into her again, I couldn't be nasty to her. She looked far from well. I said, 'What's the matter with you?'

She said, 'Only a headache. When I get one, it practically lays me out. Not to worry.'

I felt her forehead and it was quite

hot. 'You'd better go and see Home Sister. Go on! We get into awful trouble if we're under the weather and don't go to her.'

'Why?' she asked me.

Her eyes looked dark with pain so I explained. 'Because someone once thought she'd be very brave and bear up and didn't realize she was sickening for something and it was contagious and the whole of the Nurses' Home was laid low. There was awful trouble, so I'm told!' So Heather took the hint and went to Home Sister.

She was packed off to bed for the rest of the day but when I went to find Richard, it was to discover that he had swapped with someone else, so that he could have the week-end off. No doubt to take Heather out somewhere special, I thought bitterly.

I went out with Frances Trepple, who had managed to get time off. At the moment our ward wasn't too much run off its feet, so we went to the pictures and saw the whole of the main film for once and had sickly ice cream that cost more than it was worth, and then we went into a tea shop and had tea and sticky buns and talked about Heather. And oddly enough, we didn't tear her to pieces, but concentrated on her good points.

'Will you tell me, Fran,' I said, in some desperation, 'why when I'm on my own I think murderous thoughts about that girl, and when I am with someone else, I find everyone is pointing out what a nice nature she has?'

'Well, you seem to have had bad luck since you took her over,' Frances admitted thoughtfully. 'And I do admit that she has a neat technique for getting her own way without it being too obvious, but I suppose she's had to fight her way and she's found that her method of getting things is the best way for her.'

But that didn't help me. 'Fran, have you ever seen Richard's uncle, face to face, I mean?'

'Sir Russington?' She looked surprised. 'Good heavens, no, and I hope I never do!'

'But you have been sent to the Path. Lab. sometimes, haven't you? With things?'

'You know I have! We all have! But he's usually in the holy of holies, that nasty little room that everyone says don't go near.'

'Well, he was outside in the Lab. itself yesterday and he was all hunched over the test tubes and he was positively rude to me!'

'What did he look like?' she asked, really wanting to know.

'That's just it — he kept in the dark. I only saw part of his white coat in the pool of light. Oh, and he's got thick rimmed glasses.'

'Then that wasn't him,' Frances said positively. 'That sounds like Professor Westfield.'

'Is he rude?' I asked.

'Certainly is!' she averred, so then I didn't know what to think. 'But,' she said, on consideration, 'not as rude as

Sir Russington. You know, I've always wondered if there's a *reason* for all this business of his keeping out of sight. I've heard others talk about it, and at one time we used to scare ourselves with the thought that he might be awfully ugly, or perhaps — well, you know how people have accidents in Lab experiments and get scars and things — what do you think?'

I gasped. Such a thought took my breath away. 'Well, he certainly kept hidden, whoever he was,' I began, but Frances laughed.

'Aren't we a couple of idiots, hazarding guesses? When all you have to do is to ask your Richard!'

My laughter died. 'He isn't my Richard, and anyway, don't be silly. How could I possibly go up to Richard and say, 'Is your uncle ugly or scarred from an accident?'

'No, of course you can't,' she agreed. 'What about the porters? They'd know, surely. Old Gibson has been here for years!'

'Yes, but you can't gossip to porters about the Great Man. Besides, I might not be here long enough for that. Unless it was someone else and not him that I saw, then I shall certainly be out on my ear for answering him like that.'

I closed that conversation but I could see Frances wasn't going to let it remain shut for long. She'd find out, somehow. Meantime there was this business of Heather.

'Did you know she was going around with David Stanton?' I asked her.

Frances said, 'My dear, that's old hat! That only lasted three days! It's Charlie Ross now.'

'Another houseman!'

'Yes, and he *was* seeing quite a bit of that pretty staff nurse on Josiah Ward. Oh, aren't men stupid? Just because Heather's so pretty — '

'Do you really think she's pretty?' I asked bleakly.

'Well, yes, I suppose I do, but she's so modest about it. She's always saying she isn't pretty.'

Yes, that was the way she did it, I thought bitterly. And then we both looked at each other and said at the same time: 'Heather! Heather would know what he looks like!'

Just that small thing changed the tenor of the day and we were our old happy selves again. I almost forgot how Richard had gone over to Heather's side. I was just happy that I wouldn't have to ask him what his uncle looked like. Though Frances did say in perplexity, 'After all, you know the family — did you never see that uncle before?' But I had to admit that Big Shots like him didn't go out to a place like our village or stay in the rather hectic house of the local G.P.

Heather didn't keep her promise and leave the hospital, as I had known she wouldn't. She came down to my room that night. Second-years had a small slip of a room each, rather like a ship's cabin, everything built in, and just enough room to wash and get into bed, and of course, to sit at the three-drawer knee-hole contraption that did duty as dressing-table and desk in one. There certainly wasn't room for a restless young thing like Heather in it. I said, 'Look, if you're going to stay in here, sit on the bed and keep still,' and she said, 'Isn't it poky? I was miserable sharing a room with two other people but at least we've got room to *move*!'

'And you're not really supposed to come down to this floor and visit me. Was it something urgent, Heather?'

If someone had sounded cross like that to me, I'd have taken the hint and gone, but Heather looked dotingly at me and said, 'You are good to me, Eileen. Why are you? I've been nothing but trouble to you since we first met haven't I?'

She could take my breath away more easily than anyone I knew. 'No, of course you haven't,' I heard myself saying weakly.

'Well, what about Richard?'

'What about him?' I asked crossly.

'I sometimes think I am stepping in

between you both. Am I?'

Some instinct, or perhaps it was just good old pride, made me deny such a thing. 'Oh, don't be silly, Heather! We've been brought up together, that's all. He's almost family.'

'Oh.' I fancied I detected a bit of disappointment there, but I couldn't think why. She rushed on, 'Then I haven't come between you! Then it's all right. Because he's really only a friend to me, you know. He's too old to be a boyfriend.'

'Really!' I said, tartly. But I was thinking of Richard's uncle and the mystery about him and she was here and had interrupted my lecture note-taking, so I asked bluntly, 'Richard's uncle, how would you describe him?'

'Describe him?' she said, and looked scared. 'Oh, I couldn't — I'm no good at describing people.'

'But you have seen him, in the daylight, I mean?'

She licked her lips. 'Why do you ask, Eileen?'

'Because we poor mortals have never been privileged to have a good look at him but he seems to be on good enough terms with you to demand to know why you didn't take that file to him and I've just remembered he said you were to go and see him *stat*.'

'Well, why didn't you say so before?' She was outraged. 'I'd better go, then!'

'Where?' I asked sweetly. 'He takes himself off and they lock up the Path. Lab. after a certain hour, unless Professor Westfield is working late.'

'Then I'll leave it till tomorrow and I'll have to tell him you didn't give me the message, but you won't mind me doing that, will you?' she said, happily. 'You're such a kind person, though why you pretend to be cross with me all the time, I can't think.'

'Never mind that!' I snapped. 'What — is — he — like?'

'Who?' she asked blankly.

'Sir Russington!'

'Oh, that old man!' She sounded so disgusted. 'Just because he said it would be all right for Matron to take me on — '

'But why should he? Did he know you before you came here?'

'Of course not!' she said. 'Why should he?'

'Because it's very queer that he should recommend a girl he had never heard of before, that's why!'

'Well, I expect Richard asked him to recommend me,' she said simply, and I went hot with fury, because that simple explanation had completely escaped me, as it had escaped everyone else. All this mystery, wondering what the connection was between Richard's uncle and Heather! It must have been just as Jeff had said, and he ought to know his boss.

Jeff! Jeff would know what he looked like! Why hadn't I thought of asking him? Well, of course, the answer was clear — because I had been so furious with Jeff that I couldn't even be civil to him.

But I would tomorrow! That's where

I'd go, to find Jeff. If Richard was going to be out with Heather again, then I'd find out about his beastly uncle.

Heather, however, had other ideas. 'What I really came to ask you was, Eileen, if you really haven't a boy-friend and only go out with other girls, could you go with me tomorrow?'

'I thought you were booked up for tomorrow!' I exploded.

She tied her hankie into knots and untied them, making a business of it. The hankie in itself reminded me about washing the one Jeff had lent me. I should have taken it back all nice and clean today. I got up to find it and couldn't. Heather watched me, and said at last, 'Well, I know why I go out with boys, but not because I want to — they are so nice to me and they keep asking me and it would look odd if I said no and then went out by myself which we aren't supposed to do, or if I broke into other girls' groups which I would be doing because they're all close little groups in our lot — oh, Eileen, I'd like to go out with you, I really would!'

'All right, one day, but not tomor-row,' I said firmly. I had to make a promise to myself sooner or later, that Heather wouldn't just stampede over the small things I wanted to do, let alone the big important things, like buying a birthday gift for Richard's father.

'Well, what will you do tomorrow?' she asked.

'Something I have to think about and I don't want anyone with me,' I said firmly.

'Well, I'll be as quiet as a mouse,' she promised. 'I won't talk. You won't know I'm with you.'

'That I won't, because you won't be with me,' I said firmly. But I was miserable for the rest of the evening, because she got up at that, with a choking sound like a strangled sob and went out of my room without a word. What could you do with a girl like that? At least five people drifted into my room, afterwards, all saying much the same thing: 'That poor Heather child, what made her run crying out of your room, Eileen? What did you *say* to her?'

It was five days later, before I got out. Out of the hospital grounds, that is. Purposely I took my notes and sat on a seat in the small garden round the chapel, just to keep Heather away. Richard was on duty in the afternoons, I thought sourly, or else she would have been with him, though why she had deserted David Stanton and Charlie Ross, I had no idea.

It came to me, as I sat thinking, the day before I finally escaped her, that she just had to bend people to her will. She was like that. It was a game, a way of life to her, to make people do what they didn't want to do, just to please her own whim, and she had to make it appear quite unapparent what she was doing. I reflected that it could very well be a game, and a very entertaining one.

One day when I couldn't escape her, I tried to turn the tables on her by asking to hear what she had been learning. But that didn't work. She kept turning the conversation round to how I spent my free time and what my home was like and what I did with Richard when we were at home at the same time. I was quite exhausted when the session came to an end. It was stalemate. I didn't manage to keep her to reciting her notes, but neither did she manage to get much out of me, about my private life. But she appeared to know a lot about it so I supposed Richard had told her. That didn't please me either.

I dodged her by the simple means of finding out when her times changed. I chose a day when the newest batch of students were taken to see how the new hygienic methods of farm-running compared with the old-fashioned farms. That would be nice for Heather! Unless there was a good-looking unattached farmer she would be bored to tears.

Jeff wasn't where I expected to find him at all. He was in the sea. A very powerful swimmer indeed. I had been watching the man for some time, between scouring the shore for a sight of Jeff, and then I realized that the swimmer was him! Well, I should have known! Those powerful muscles rippled as he moved. He was evenly tanned all over, and there was not a single wasted movement as he cut through what was by no means a smooth sea. In fact, there weren't many swimmers out.

He must have caught sight of me at once, as he stood up to come out. He quickly rubbed down, and pulled slacks and sweater over his swimming trunks, having waved to me to make sure I knew he had seen me. I just curtly nodded back at him but I waited for him.

I stood at the top of the steps with the intention of talking to him there. I worked it out that if he stood a couple of steps below me, I'd be an inch or two above him and wouldn't feel inferior. But it didn't work out like that. He just took my elbows and gently moved me to one side, and came to the top, and there was a mischievous twinkle in his eyes as he said, 'You were waiting for me. Now what on earth has gone wrong for you to want to speak to the dogs-body of the formidable uncle of your fella?'

I could have hit him. 'I have only one question I wanted to ask you, Jeff,' I said. Then I went red. I hadn't meant to use his name. 'What's your other name?' I demanded.

'What other name?' he asked, but I'd wiped the smile off.

'Your surname, of course. I know you're Jeff, but Jeff what?'

He decided to look delighted. 'Clever girl, that's *it*!'

'What's it?' I said irritably. He had moved me along so that he could lean on the rails above the beach, and watch my every change of expression. I tried turning away from him but the wind hit me clean between the eyes, stinging my face with flying sand particles. Not a pleasant day to stand talking to someone like this man who didn't seem to mind the elements and was always happy and comfortable.

He sighed. 'You asked me my name, then you guessed it,' he explained patiently. 'Jeff Watt.'

I gasped. 'I don't believe it! You're just being . . . facetious.'

He sighed again. 'Well, if you're not going to believe it, why ask what my name is?'

'Well, I must call you something!'

'Jeff, then,' he said, as if tired of the subject. 'Now, what did you want me for?'

His impatient tone nettled me. 'Just one thing,' I snapped. 'Tell me what your boss looks like.'

It sounded pretty silly the minute I'd said it, but I'm sure it didn't merit the surprise, the creasing up of his face into a look of unholy glee nor was it necessary for him to throw back his head and laugh. It gave me a chance to see just how good-looking he was, in case I hadn't noticed it before. His perfect teeth were shining white against the even tan of his skin, and he didn't carry an ounce of excess flesh. All muscle, perfectly formed, all male and very conscious of it. Well, why wouldn't he be? All the girls looked at him with approval as they went by, and he was aware of that, too. His hair crisply waved, all short to his head, glistening with droplets of water still in it. His brows were dead straight and shining black, and his lashes were black enough to make any girl wild with envy. And his mouth was a very nice shape indeed . . . if you liked that sort of mouth, I thought angrily. I was much more conscious of the cleft in that extremely determined chin of his.

'When you've finished enjoying yourself, perhaps you'll answer the question,' I said acidly.

'Let's walk. It's chilly,' he said, and took my elbow, and I couldn't shake him off. 'Don't be pettish,' he reproved. 'Surely in these democratic days you won't mind walking with me, while you pick my brains about my boss?' and he grinned at me in the most aggravating manner.

'I only want to know what he looks like,' I persisted.

'Tell me why, first,' he said.

'Why should I?'

'Because I'm your last hope, I should think, or you'd never have asked me. For some reason, nobody else will satisfy your curiosity.'

'Really, you're the limit! I am going to be hauled over the coals and I want to know which man to avoid making another gaffe with, the next time I'm sent to the Path. Lab.,' I said hotly.

'Simple,' Jeff said expansively. 'Just be polite to them all.'

He stopped at a stall serving tea. 'Want some? Well, I could do with a cup, so you don't mind standing by me while I drink it if you won't join me?' So I said I'd like one too, and there was a short struggle over who would pay, and finally he gave in. 'All right, if you're so flush, you can pay for both of us,' he said handsomely.

Oh, I could have hit him! He said, 'Now the way I see it is, you've already come to the conclusion that the little bent chap with thick glasses in the corner was the Big Shot. Now you want to know how old he is, and what his habits are when off duty. Right?'

'Nothing of the sort!' I flared. 'I don't care what he does off duty. Anyway, I know, don't I, that he goes sailing.' I thought a bit. 'He can't be so old and bent, to take charge of a big craft like the *Seamaid II*,' I said at last, and I suppose my tone shook him into making an admission.

'What do you think I'm here for, if not to handle that craft?' and he sounded so surprised that I thought, I must have been right at first. Richard's uncle must be quite old. Besides, to be such a Big Shot in that field, he couldn't be anything else but old. All the professors and senior staff had white hair, well, grey, anyway, and lined faces. When one has so much to do with the sick and the injured, and the people at the top who have spent a lifetime getting there, learning the best way to treat them, gosh, one does love the sight of strong whole flesh, energetic healthy limbs, the smooth contours of a young face, the bright blue tinge in the whites of young eyes. And this man's strength and animal love of life was contagious. He made me feel I wanted to be in that icy sea, or running with him along the edge of the shore, where the outgoing tide had left the surface fine and hard and changing colour as the wet seeped out of it. He made me think of fine weather and winds over the heath, and walking on air and excitement in just being alive.

I pulled myself up sharply, and in a way I was puzzled, as I remembered that never once, in all the best times I had had with Richard, had he made me feel like this. Richard wasn't excessively given to physical exercise. He'd much rather cycle or drive than walk or run or climb. I was the lunatic who liked doing those things. But Richard had other qualities that the dogsbody of his uncle simply hadn't got; couldn't possibly have, I firmly told myself.

'So . . . he's not young enough to wrestle with a 45-footer,' I said. 'And he wears glasses and has grey hair — how old is he?'

'Why don't you ask him, the next time you go in for six of the best for being cheeky?' he asked, laughing. 'Well, you told me yourself that you answered back! What can you expect? Oh, do let's forget about him and talk about something else,' he urged. 'You swim, don't you?'

'What makes you think I do?' I countered, wondering how I could put the question I so badly wanted the answer to: was the uncle of Richard scarred in any way? It would be so futile if I had to concede to Frances that I couldn't find out anyhow, because Frances really thought that if I was as close to Richard as *I* thought I was, then the question should be simple and easy.

As I should have agreed about, I suppose, if I hadn't been so miserable about Richard. What made someone like Richard fall in love with someone like Heather, who went out with so many young men and had them all falling head over heels in love with her?

Jeff broke into my thoughts by saying, 'The critical way you were watching me.' He said it so calmly, and of course it was true. 'Come swimming with me tomorrow — or are you scared to?'

'I'm terrified,' I said calmly, spiking his guns. If he thought I'd scramble for a date swimming with him just because he was so good-looking, he was wrong.

He finished his tea and got up to go. I hastily put my cup down. He looked down at me and took my arm again. Somehow, now he wasn't wearing the dirty cords and jersey, he didn't look like anyone's dogsbody. 'I wish you would, Eileen,' he said. 'I'd like you to come swimming with me. I think we'd have fun, especially in a sea like that!'

I was so tempted. I knew I'd have fun with him. But I wouldn't go. And it wasn't because of Richard, either.

Jeff said, 'You don't want to go swimming with someone's dogsbody!' and it was an accusation.

'Oh, don't be silly,' I said impatiently. 'It's not that at all!'

'Then what is it?' he asked. And as we'd somehow arrived at the end of the promenade, and the people had thinned out to almost half a dozen, he took me by the shoulders and made me face him. 'You owe it to me to tell me!'

'Why do I? I don't owe you anything. Besides, you won't answer my question about your boss!'

'Oh, that! I did answer it — I'm no good at describing, and who cares? What do you want to know about *him* for? Think about me — swimming with me. Go on, give it a whirl! Bet you'd beat you out to the Point.'

'No,' I said.

After a pause, he said, 'Well, at least tell me why. Someone else? It *is* dear little Richard Barclay, isn't it?'

I turned on him, in fury. He laughed, still holding me by the arms, and said, 'Sorry, sorry, I take it back — *if* you give me the real reason,' and his grip on me hurt. I'd be bruised, but there was something else, too. Something that bothered me much more. I had been pleasantly conscious of Richard's arm round my waist or shoulders in the past, but now I was learning from this man that there are many different kinds of contact, even with the grip of a man's hands on the upper arms. It was how I imagined an electric shock would feel, ripping through one. I just wanted him to take his hands off me, and my ever-ready temper rising, I snapped back the truth at him. At least it made him drop his hands.

'My Gran,' I said tartly, 'has always warned me not to join in the race for some man, with the pretty girls. She made me realize at a very early age that

I am plain. See?'

His smile left his face, and he looked oddly at me. Surprised, too, I suppose, perhaps because he hadn't expected that answer.

'And don't think I mind not being pretty,' I added. 'I just want to enjoy life and good health and be a good nurse and — and — '

What else did I want? Just then, I couldn't have said, in so many words, but now I was conscious of a curious aching yearning, of wanting something that I couldn't put a name to. Of being vaguely unhappy because it was just eluding me, all the time. I told myself firmly that it was Richard, but there was a nagging feeling that that might have been the truth once, but was not any longer and that had a queer upsetting effect on me, too. It was as if I had suddenly become a stranger to myself, a stranger I had no hope of understanding.

He put his hand in the pocket of his slacks and pulled out a small battered leather pocket-book. He opened it and took out of one of the compartments a very much creased coloured picture, about two inches square. Oh, no, I thought, he isn't going to show me the one girl he cares for, surely? That would be adding insult to injury.

He held it out to me. 'Remember that?' and I recognized it.

'Hey, how did you get hold of that?' I demanded and tried to take it from him, but he held it beyond my reach.

'It's mine,' he said. 'Since the day I picked it up. You relinquished all claim on it when you screwed it up and threw it away in disgust. Remember that day? You were with two other nurses, and they were squealing with girlish laughter, having their pictures done in a cabinet on the front.'

'Yes, I remember,' I agreed. 'I threw it away because it made me look plainer than I really am. It was silly, anyway, getting it done, but they wanted to. But that's no reason for you to pick it up and keep it.' And I glared at the picture he still held; A square face with a short comic nose and a mouth a little too wide for my taste, and brown eyes; topped by a short cut, like a boy's — brown hair that the wind flicked up. All brown. Plain.

'I don't see why not,' Jeff objected. Then, in a more persuading tone, he abandoned the question of the picture which he put away, and urged, 'I'm only asking you to come swimming with me! Go on, be a sport. I work pretty hard, and people aren't always nice to me, and I've always thought you were a decent sort — fair-minded, that sort of thing.'

Yes, that's what Gran always said of me. Cheerful, if possessing a bad temper, but I never sulk. Fair-minded, good-natured, the lot — everything in fact except pretty, charming, alluring, all the things a girl wants to be if she isn't.

I shrugged. 'Okay, I'll come swimming, so long as it's clearly understood,'

I finished fiercely, 'that I am not compet-ing with the Dollies who smirk at you going along, and that I do not agree with them that you're good-looking or . . . or any of the daft things they are obviously thinking about you.'

He was shaking with silent laughter, but he cooled down and threw a matey arm round my shoulders. 'Thank you, Eileen, for that speech,' he said, still hard put to it to be serious. 'It will be nice, I don't mind telling you, to go swimming with someone who's think-ing about speed and technique and . . . nothing else.'

Funny, how chilling I found that remark of his.

3

It rained next day and was very cold, and Richard decided that we should go and choose his father's pipe.

Funny, how weather doesn't matter, when you're with the person who means most to you. It had all the elements of a wonderful day about it. Heather wasn't free and I was in Richard's car. It didn't matter that it was so cold that everyone had deserted the town. It didn't matter to me that the wind drove the rain before it so that one could see, actually see, the sharp needles of water that stabbed furiously at the pavements from the lowering black clouds. Richard, who hated driving in the rain, muttered under his breath, but we had cut it too fine to do anything else but go shopping today.

There was a pipe shop that was literally a dream of a place. We spent far too long in there, choosing and discarding. The smell of the tobaccos was dreamy, too. Richard bought a pipe for himself, and only the thought that his father wouldn't use it, stopped us from buying a pipe lying in a velvet-lined case. How can one small briar pipe make such an ordinary wet windy day into a dream period? I know I beamed at everyone because I caught sight of my silly face in one of the mirrors in the shop. The chap behind the counter beamed on me and referred to me as Richard's 'young lady', which I think is a very nice term, and Richard didn't deny it. I think he was thinking about something else at the time, but I wouldn't dwell on that.

After that, we went to our favourite place and had tea. Not just a pot of tea, but cream to go in it, and cream buns and splits, and home-made jam, the lot. One thing about Richard, he adores food as I do, and he did justice to that meal.

Richard didn't mention Heather, and

I was careful of my tongue and never mentioned her, either. I didn't even think of his terrible uncle. I just enjoyed that time with him. Rather like a schoolgirl, I suppose.

When we'd cleaned up the plates, he sat back, replete, and grinned at me. 'Aren't we awful,' he said softly. 'Stuffing all this — would you like me to order some more cakes?'

'Richard!' I exploded.

'Don't say you're slimming,' he begged me. 'Never you!' and I agreed: 'No, I don't have to. I can eat as much as I like. And I'm always hungry.'

'Well, they don't give you girls enough to eat,' he agreed.

'Oh, I don't know,' I murmured. I didn't even mind talking shop, I was so happy.

'How's that ward of yours?' he asked suddenly. 'Not overworking, are you?' and I told him I wasn't, and that I found it very absorbing.

Then the bombshell exploded. So quietly, I didn't expect it and hardly noticed it, when it happened. 'No, you take it in your stride — it almost agrees with you, ward work, no matter how hard it is. But I don't mind telling you, I'm worried about Heather. What's it going to be like for a girl like her, put on to a ward like yours, for instance?'

I sat back, the smile wiped off my face. So, all the time, all the time he had been apparently enjoying this blissful afternoon with me, he had been thinking about Heather! I said, 'I expect she'll survive, or leave. She threatens to leave sometimes, when things don't go her way. But she rides the storm.'

He looked at me. I gritted my teeth and wondered dully how I would ever be able to control that tongue of mine, now or at any future time. Again I had said the wrong thing and he was shocked. He looked it. He said he was.

'How can you talk about a girl like Heather in that way?' he whispered. 'You don't even like her, do you?'

Well, the damage was done. I lost my temper completely. 'Oh, be your age,

71

Richard! Grow up! You may be soppy over Heather, but I'm not and no other girl is! We preserve a healthy outlook towards each other, and we see each other as we really are! No, I don't dislike Heather, though there are times when I wonder why I don't. But I don't. Perhaps I don't care about any girl enough to dislike her, or to like her, for that matter. I care about my work, my patients, and if someone like Heather finds she can't stand the pace, then she'd better find work elsewhere. And she'd be the first to concede that, in case you didn't know!'

He just sat shaking his head. 'I never thought you'd be like that, Eileen! I thought you liked her specially! She says you do!'

'Does she indeed?' I gathered my things together. 'Thank you for the tea, Richard, but I really think we'd better be getting back. Don't you?'

He agreed about that, but not without reluctance. I think, looking back, that after having eaten ourselves silly, he was ready to sit and have a nice cosy natter about Heather, with me. And he couldn't even see that I naturally didn't want to discuss Heather.

His car wouldn't start, and we had to walk back. At least, we would have had to, if David Stanton hadn't given us a lift. He, too, wanted to talk about Heather. I wondered how Richard would take it, young Stanton being so gooey about her, but he settled down to a jolly discussion about what Heather wanted to do that week-end. Apparently she had expressed a wish to be taken to various shops to buy coloured paper, spangly stuff, poster paints, etc., to make a Fancy Dress.

'Oh, lord, yes, I forgot! The Fancy Dress Ball!' Richard clapped his hand to his forehead. 'You going, Eileen?'

He had forgiven me. Or forgotten what he had been angry with me about. I didn't know which and I didn't care. A cold lump of misery had settled down inside me again. It was all very well Gran giving me good advice but she hadn't taught me how to capture someone like Richard, who was already head over heels in love with one of the pretty, alluring ones.

'What for?' I asked.

'Oh, go on,' David urged, glancing dangerously over his shoulder at me. 'It's fun! The thing is, one mustn't buy a super Fancy Dress. It's got to be made up out of cheap stuff or else made over from some old thing. You want to get Heather to help you! She's got the most wonderful ideas! She's already given some to the other kids in her set. Generous to a fault, Heather!'

Richard agreed, and they discussed what she was going as. A butterfly, it seemed. Well, that suited her, I told myself rather bitterly. 'What will you go as, Eileen?' Richard broke off to ask.

'A tramp, I daresay. A lady tramp. Then I can wear the old clothes I usually go out in, without making much effort.' I said.

David took that as a great joke and

roared with laughter, and looked over his shoulder at us, so that we careered at a slant and almost hit a lamp-post. Richard said a few things to him so he didn't do that again. But the Fancy Dress Ball was still the topic of conversation when we got back to the hospital.

Of course, it's sense to get up Fancy Dress from nothing at all. It isn't as easy as just ordering a Fancy Dress. The ideas I heard about were really very good. Frances decided to go as a house with the roof as a hat. After she had done her lecture notes, she painstakingly painted lines of red bricks from a child's paint box, on cardboard from a stocking box. It was rather clever, really, the way she worked it out. Others were jostling for the two hand-sewing-machines. Another nurse on our floor, who came from Jamaica, decided to go in a bikini with a skirt of raffia and lots of beads with ear-rings made of two big curtain rings, tied on her ears. 'Well, I don't care if I *don't* have to put burnt cork all over me!' she giggled. 'It isn't cheating — it's just common sense.' And amid laughter, we all agreed with her. She would be terrific.

But nobody could think what I could go as. Heather worked on her paints and glitter, and somehow she managed to get the front of her hair bleached to a golden shaft, and when she had a dress rehearsal, even I had to admit that from the basest materials and a lot of imagination and skill, she had really thought up a glamorous costume. Everyone said so. She had a way of standing, that was all allure, and with her arms held up, opening out the wings, she was terrific.

I said I'd go as a surgeon, borrowing one of the white coats and holding a saw and scalpel, but nobody would have have that. 'Cheating!' they roared, so I ventured the idea of a sweep — all I'd have to do would be to get some soot from the boiler room and cover myself in it, but that was vetoed. I'd make everyone I touched in a shocking mess. Daily I came up with a half-satirical idea, not really meaning to go, so what did the costume matter? Richard was only going because of Heather. Whether I was jealous or not, didn't seem to make much difference. I would have no partner — she'd have him!

It was in this frame of mind that I next saw Jeff. He was coming out of a chemist's in the High Street, looking at some films he had got. The sun was blinding that day, after rain, so I wasn't entirely surprised to find him with dark glasses on, but I recognized him. How, I wondered afterwards? He was in different clothes — a rather neat dark suit, one that a person wouldn't remember afterwards — the sort that Gran labelled 'the attire of a gentle-man' because you didn't remember details afterwards, only the general impression that he was very well dressed. One of his boss's cast-off suits, I thought sourly, and then amended that. He wouldn't be able to get his big frame into one of that rude little man's suits!

I almost forgot that I wanted him. I ran after him, shouting 'Jeff! Hey, wait for me!' and he stopped in surprise and waited for me.

'How did you recognize me?' he asked in some surprise.

Well, how, I asked myself? Perhaps by his walk, the way he threw his head back, to look above the crowds. Well, he could, he was so tall.

I said, 'I don't know, but I do know it's you!' and I wondered why I suddenly felt all fussed, as if I'd been running, caught out in something, not exactly embarrassed or excited, but just, well, upset. I didn't like it, unreasonably blamed him for it, and thrust a small paper packet at him. 'Here, this is what I wanted to give you — the hankie you lent me. I've washed and ironed it.'

He seemed oddly touched and didn't seem to know what to say. He just stood looking at it. So I said impatiently,

'Well, got lots to do so I must push off now. Okay?'

He took my arm by way of reply. He was so strong, sparks went up to the top of my head and back again. I wrenched myself free, and he chose to ignore that, saying calmly, 'Thank you, Eileen, for the labour on the hankie. Do me a favour, will you? I've got an awful problem. The Big Boss wants to give Assistant Matron a birthday token. Last year he got flowers for her, and didn't know they gave her an allergy.'

'Ass. Mat. — *flowers?*' My good humour was restored. It was three-fold restoration: the thought of the acidular Assistant Matron receiving a birthday token from Old Meanie, for a start; the thought that he hadn't bothered to find out first if she'd got anything peculiar, and she had, for a second thing; and the third — oh, gorgeous, the mere thought that old Cleverpants Jeff Watt had the unenviable job of getting the token this year! I laughed silently but hurtingly. He said sharply, 'Let's get inside this restaurant, before you disgrace me further in the High Street!' and he marched me to a quiet table in the corner.

But he wasn't a bad sort. He had a laugh at himself when I explained, although the laughter had a wry touch about it which I didn't understand. Well, it can't be much fun being the Big Shot's dogsbody, when you're young and healthy and strong and handsome. I wondered fleetingly how much he was paid, then decided I didn't care enough. I undertook to tell him one or two things he might get for Ass. Mat., like, for instance, her passion for a certain toilet water fitted with a spray, and called the unlikely name of 'Beechwoods in Autumn', and the name finished him. He, however, managed to smother his laughter, though he looked as if he were going to have apoplexy.

In the end he said, 'Thanks for the hint, but it will hardly do. I mean, how would the Big Boss be expected to know that? Or on the other hand, the fact that he'd managed to find out might suggest a secret passion for the lady and that would never do!' and that set me off laughing again. It was a very merry coffee morning, and I had honestly enjoyed it.

'But why does he give her a birthday present if he isn't that way about her?' I asked, on a sudden thought.

He looked quizzically at me. 'Don't you honestly know, Eileen? Her father had a lot to do with the hospital. He was a surgeon, they tell me. All the top brass give her a little something, and it's special because the Fancy Dress Ball will be held on that date.'

'Oh.' My fun died. I didn't want to be reminded of that.

'No ideas for a Fancy Dress?' he guessed. 'Shall I give you one or two?'

'No, thanks,' I said shortly, and got up. 'I shan't be going.'

'You will, you know,' he reminded me, getting smartly to his feet too. 'Everyone has to go. I just told you. It's

Ass. Mat.'s birthday. It would look very rude not to go, unless I'd strangled you or someone else had!' and he was grinning broadly.

'Well, I'll think of something,' I said crossly.

'Go as an urchin, Eileen,' he coaxed. 'Go on! Oldest jeans and jersey — the ones I've seen you wear with great fervour — and make your face dirty, roughen your hair, and wear an old cap backwards. The boilerman's got one he'll let you have, I know!'

'How do you know?' I asked suspiciously.

He shrugged. 'I suppose I might be called an employee of the hospital, wouldn't you say?'

'Oh, yes, on account of your boss,' I mused, and found he was looking all twinkling and amused at me. I suppose because I'd been in such bad odour with his beastly boss, and I was scared of him.

'Well, I'll think about the costume. And thanks,' I said grudgingly. 'Yes, I'll do that,' I finished handsomely, as I told myself he wouldn't be there to see if I did what he suggested or not.

Heather grabbed me on my return and said she had just the thing for me. Among her perculiar clothes she had favoured before coming to the hospital was, she told me, a grey gown. She announced it with such pride that it rather cut the ground from my feet. 'Come and see it!' she begged, and when we opened the battered old case, there was a smell of things like in a theatrical props hamper. Half scenty, half stale, half dusty; oh, an odd but rather special sort of smell one connects with the theatre. 'What is it?' I asked, as she dragged out what looked like thin grey wisps.

She held it up. 'An afternoon frock of my aunt's. It's called tulle, only it's gone a bit limp. It's perfect for the purpose, honestly, Eileen! Look,' and she held it up against me.

Perfect, I thought bitterly. Grey's my worst colour. 'What am I supposed to be — a ghost?' I asked glumly.

'Well, that's an idea, only actually, no, I thought of a pair — you be a moth to my butterfly.'

I looked at her. She seemed so utterly pleased with herself to have thought of such a thing. 'Look, I made this — it took me all afternoon yesterday, and it's a surprise!' She held up a wire ring to go round my head, with glass beads called bugles, stuck all round and two antennae covered in glass beads. 'There! I'm the Golden Butterfly and you're the little Grey Moth!' she said, and she honestly thought that was fine. You could see it. Then she frowned. 'Oh, your hair. It's too dark and springy for a moth.'

'I'm sure you could find a Granny wig for me,' I said bitterly.

'No, but you've reminded me of something,' and she rummaged in her trunk and brought out a little grey furry cap which appeared to completely cover my hair. She was so enthusiastic about it that she called other people in before

I could stop her, and as they were the youngest of the lot, it wasn't funny.

I said crossly, 'That'll do, Heather! I'm not supposed to be up here, anyway. Help me take the stuff off!'

She looked at her friends for confirmation, and I could see they were thinking what I was thinking. But not Heather. She appealed to them. Didn't they think we made a wonderful pair?

'I'm not going, anyway,' I said. 'You didn't even ask me or I could have told you!'

Heather looked near to tears, and her friends, clustered by the door watching us, suddenly turned on me, so that when she said in a wobbly voice, 'But I gave up my afternoon yesterday to make it for you!' they took up the chant, and someone added, from the safety of the back, that Second Years were all alike, the way they treated the girls in the Training School.

It was a foregone conclusion. It only wanted for her to tell Richard, and then I would indeed be in bad odour all round, so I gave in. Not specially because I cared what Richard would say about this but because she had, after all, given up her time and stayed in. Heather couldn't bear to be kept in. I had discovered that, very early on. It was a sort of claustrophobia. She had to get out.

Anyway, they were making such a racket that eventually Home Sister came along, before I could struggle out of the wretched thing. Heather was trying to keep my arms out. She had fastened the cloying folds of the grey tulle to my wrists, and she pushed my arms up and said, 'Look, Sister, isn't it nice? Nurse Amberley's said she'll go as a moth, to my butterfly!'

I gave up. But Sister didn't say a thing or two to me for being in the centre of all that row, on the wrong floor. She just looked thoughtfully at me and said, 'I see.'

The other girls shrilled, 'Heather *made* it for Nurse Amberley, in her *time off*, Sister!' and again Home Sister looked thoughtful at me and said, 'Very nice.'

But after I had got out of the thing and escaped, I found Sister pushing some flower stalks in different places in a vase in the corridor window, and she turned as she heard me. 'Nurse Amberley,' she began. Wait for it, I thought! But she merely said mildly, 'I am very pleased to see you are extending friendship to Nurse Maple. More pleased than I can say. Your brisk and healthy attitude to life is just what that young woman wants.'

I could only say weakly, 'Really, Sister? Thank you, Sister!' and totter away, feeling an absolute heel. Well, wasn't that the way Heather always left one feeling?

She attached herself to me next morning when I went shopping and because of what Home Sister had said, I didn't feel I could get rid of her, and I was rather annoyed, because I saw Jeff Watt in the High Street again, and he hastily put on his dark glasses and turned away, but he looked annoyed, too. I suppose he wanted to give me more advice about what sort of costume he thought I should wear. Well, bully for everyone! I should look terrible, anyway, it seemed. So why worry?

Heather had a problem. There was a boy, it seemed, from her old life. 'I *would* like to see him, just for old time's sake, Eileen, but he *can't* come to the hospital because of reasons. I thought, if we could *meet* him somewhere — '

'Why drag me into it?' I asked in amazement. 'Why don't you take one of your friends with you?'

'Because Home Sister says she feels safer if I'm out with you,' Heather said simply. And that rather clinched the matter. Of course, they were a harum-scarum lot in Heather's set. And there was always, I reminded myself, Richard's terrible uncle behind it all. If anything happened to Heather, I suppose everyone would be blamed. Always, that *reason* for his interest in

Heather, cropped up and worried me. I didn't believe for a moment that his servant would know the real reason, so I discounted what Jeff had said. I said pretty sharply to Heather, 'Just how well do you know this uncle of Richard's? And don't evade the issue this time!'

Heather opened her eyes to their widest extent. 'Oh, but I don't. Like I told you before. I don't know him at all well!'

'Then why did he speak for you, to Matron?' I pressed.

'*Did* he?' she asked, in just such a tone that I could have shaken her. 'Well, I have heard it said that he probably did it to please your Richard, who is as kind as you are, Eileen, but I don't know, of course.' And there she had me. Confirmation of the very thing I had feared. Richard had asked his uncle to get her in, but for form's sake had had to make it appear that I was the one who had wanted her! Oh, I saw it all very clearly then, and I hated Richard's uncle for being so obliging to his dear nephew.

And then the Fancy Dress Ball was on us. All of a rush. It was held in the big room at the back of the Nurses' Home — a room that could close down into four decent-sized rooms, or have partitions pushed back and make a really big one. There was one off this for refreshments; and the Christmas, Easter, and Summer 'do's' and anything we got up for various charities, were all held here. It had been decorated beautifully, and everyone was keeping up that high tempo of row that people do at parties. Isn't it funny? They seem to laugh more, and talk at a higher pitch than usual, and they throw things, like streamers and bits out of bags, and they blow silly trumpets and things. And it all goes very quiet when Matron and the Big Shots come in, and everyone does a circumspect turn around the floor, following the particular Big Shot who asks Matron to dance, and of course, Ass. Mat., and Richard had declined to dress up and had come in super evening dress, with a mask on. I hadn't realized it was to be a masked ball, but it didn't matter anyway, because Heather had finally put a grey stuff 'face' over mine, with slanting holes for the eyes, and it finished just below my nose so I could talk and eat and drink, which was as well, but considering I looked terrible, I couldn't see the need to talk and surely nobody would bother to get me food and drink.

How I wished I hadn't come. Richard danced with Heather and so did David and a boy named Rod who loafed around and drooled over her, and then a succession of other people's boy-friends, because she looked so gorgeous in her costume and she really did dance divinely. I grant her that, she simply did.

I found a nice quiet place behind a stack of chairs, to lean and watch the dancers, only someone was already there, also leaning and moodily watching everyone else. His height made my heart do stupid things again, but I told myself that this couldn't be, couldn't possibly be, who I feared it was! His costume was good, whoever he was — the old-time parody of a burglar, complete with striped jersey, tight pants and sneakers, a cloth cap and neckerchief, and the inevitable black mask. As inevitable as the bag of 'swag' he now lowered to a nearby chair to turn on me and take my shoulders in hands that were familiar in their touch.

'What in the world are you supposed to be, Eileen?' he asked softly, and the part of his face below the mask didn't look pleased at all.

'What are you doing here, Jeff Watt?' I asked fiercely, but as before, he shrugged, and said, 'I told you — I'm sort of employed by the hospital, wouldn't you say?'

So I said, 'How did you know it was me?' and that seemed to give him some difficulty in answering.

'Your walk,' he said at last. 'You really should have come as an urchin. Your walk is far too cocky and fighty for a miserable grey whatever-it-is you're supposed to be! What is it, anyway?'

'A moth, to Heather's butterfly,' I said, and could have kicked myself. The way I said it sounded so mean.

He turned and looked, and found her without difficulty. She was the most brightly coloured thing there; the most striking costume, easily, and what was more, it really suited her. She *was* a golden butterfly, I thought, and hated myself for being mean to her.

'And how did you recognize me?' he asked softly, still holding my arms, which now made struggling useless.

'Take your hands off me and I'll tell you!' I flared at him, so he did, and bowed mockingly, and waited to be told. It struck me that he really wanted to know.

'I don't see why you're so interested,' I said, glumly, because now he had removed his hands, I missed the touch and wished I hadn't insisted. I was bothered, too, by this new attitude of mind of mine. It wasn't like me. I was the most practical of persons — I just fixed my sights on Richard and wanted nothing else of anyone, until this man had come into my life, and he was having such an upsetting effect, and I didn't understand it at all. 'You'll have to unmask when everyone else does,' I added.

'Oh, I know,' he said, in such a tone that I guessed in that moment that he wouldn't be there when they unmasked. I was right, then: he really had no business to be here.

'Eileen, will you dance with me?' he asked. 'Then you can tell me, without fear of embarrassment, how it was you recognized me.'

Furious, I was stung to say, 'You really are the limit! You have only one thought in your head, haven't you? 'It's a female — what does she think of me?' Well, if you want to know, I guessed that the man trying to hide behind the chairs had no business to be here and his height was yours so it wasn't so difficult.'

'Oh, is that all?' he asked mockingly, swinging me out on to the floor. They had abandoned for the moment the energetic gyrations all the young people like to do, and had reverted to a dreamy waltz with the bright lights out, and only soft blue shaded ones on. I couldn't enjoy it, he was upsetting me so. And he made matters worse by gently decreasing the distance between us and putting his face against mine. It struck me that he could surely feel the excitement or whatever it was racing through me, for he murmured, half teasingly, half tenderly, 'If you dance like this with your Richard I honestly suggest that lad wants his head examined, to keep his thoughts turned to that little butterfly, who likes 'em by the dozen.'

I gasped as if cold water had been thrown over me. 'I won't have you say things like that about Dr Barclay! You have no right, no right at all! Besides, he isn't like that.'

'If,' Jeff murmured experimentally, 'if I weren't someone's dogsbody, would you feel any different?' and the question, softly put against my ear, hung in the air. I had to answer it. He was forcing me, by the increasing pressure of those hands of his on me. And then reprieve came. It was, after all, one of those silly interruption dances, and young David Stanton, deprived of Heather, didn't really mind who he danced with, so he chose me as being the nearest.

I was glad to go, but it was only momentarily. I knew very well that Jeff Watt would have the answer from me before he slid away, probably back to the seat of his boss's car, where he should have been all this time. And what was I going to say to him? My heart pumped painfully and I tried to concentrate on Richard, and how I felt about Heather for literally brainwashing him to like her to the exclusion of everyone else. Only somehow it wouldn't work. In that moment, I couldn't even remember what Richard's face looked like!

4

Afterwards my friends wouldn't let the subject alone. To them it was an outrage, what Heather did. But it didn't surprise me. She blandly forgot that she had made such a fuss about our going to the Fancy Dress Dance as a 'double' and took the first prize all on her own.

I had to hand it to her. She scintillated. Jeff Watt had been standing near me, and I meant to keep an eye on him because I knew the exact moment when the unmasking happened. But he beat me to it. He just wasn't there. Richard was, right beside me, and at first he didn't recognize me.

He was, of course, watching Heather. She didn't just walk by in the parade as a butterfly; she threw up her arms and made the 'wings' quiver, and somehow she looked more golden than the bits and pieces of paint and tinsel merited. I found myself thinking that someone should have got her into a theatrical company. She was a born actress, because she lived the part. She wasn't really acting at all, but *being* the thing. She quivered and flitted and was all gaiety and brilliance, just like a butterfly. She enchanted everyone but somehow Richard was upset.

I said, 'Well, she deserved it, didn't she? There's nobody here to touch her, honestly, now is there?'

He looked angrily at me and said, quite unaccountably, 'Good heavens, Eileen, couldn't you do better than that thing? Didn't you *want* to look nice?'

Of course, that was how he had been over the years; the kind but sometimes scolding big brother, who wanted to be proud of me before other people. So I didn't take much notice, and shrugged. 'I wanted to please Heather, so I did as she wanted,' I said lightly. 'Goodness, I can't please everyone. I wouldn't try.'

'Heather wanted you to look like

that?' He couldn't believe it.

'I thought I told you,' I said slowly, but it didn't matter. If I had told him, I doubt if he would have listened. He was head in the clouds these days. 'What's the matter? Have you and Heather fallen out?' I asked him.

'Well, if you must know, I don't like her making an exhibition of herself like that!'

'But you know she wanted to go on the stage; it's only the sort of thing she's always wanted to do, apparently.'

Richard wasn't to be appeased. Something else had upset him. 'Who was that chap I saw you with?' he wanted to know.

'Which one?' I asked guardedly. Somehow I didn't want to discuss Jeff Watt with Richard. He would be angry, of course, that I was being friendly with his uncle's dogsbody. Besides, I didn't want to get Jeff into trouble for being at the dance when I was quite sure he had had no right to be there.

But I needn't have worried. Richard

had apparently got cross about some-one else. 'A fair chap. I think he must be one of the new dressers. You don't want to encourage that lot, Eileen!'

'Well, *you* dance with me, then,' I said, out of the depths of my misery, as the band struck up again. It was the last waltz, and I was quite well aware that he must have already asked Heather for that one. I think he had, too, for his face looked as if someone had hit him, and when I followed his glance, I saw the triumphant Heather going off with not one beau, but three, all trying to jostle for the place at her side. Richard said curtly, 'Okay, the supper dance it is!' but I don't think he enjoyed it any more than I did.

Anyway, he got called out in the middle of it, to an emergency, so I went, too. Anything to get out of that awful costume.

Heather pretended to be upset when she saw me next day. 'Eileen, where *were* you? We were supposed to be a pair! But I couldn't find you and there wasn't time to look for you! Didn't you *want* to share the prize with me?'

For sheer cheek that surpassed all, I thought, in disgust. 'I couldn't think of such a thing!' I said sardonically.

As usual there was a crowd of her friends round her, and they all said, 'Trust a second year not to want to be on hand when she was wanted! You ruined her evening!' So I looked fierce at them and they had the grace to look abashed.

'You enjoy your prize and stop being an idiot,' I told Heather, and returned the hideous moth outfit.

But Heather couldn't bear to feel she was in the wrong or that someone else wasn't getting cross with her as she deserved. She said, 'Who was the chap in the striped jersey that I saw you with? You were hidden in that corner with him for *ages*!'

'Was Richard dancing with you?' I asked her, and she admitted that at the time, he was. 'Well, then, you be satisfied, and if you'll take a bit of advice from me, settle down to work for a while now the fun's all over!'

'But I want to know — ' she said, and her broken question hung in the air.

'Why?' I snapped.

'Well, I'd like to meet him! He looks fun,' she said, and the other students clamoured for their idol to have what she was reaching for.

I don't know how I looked at her, but suddenly she laughed and retreated, but she got her own back. 'Aren't I greedy?' she said saucily. 'I've got lots of boy friends and here I am wanting poor old Eileen's one-shot thing. Well, at least, I expect it was only one-shot, wasn't it? Just for last night? Or are you meeting him again?'

'Like you said, chum, aren't you greedy,' I grinned and walked off and left them.

Heather didn't take umbrage. She was always laughing, sometimes at herself. And she was clever enough not to boast of having Richard, too, because everyone knew that Richard had been a special friend of mine before she had come.

But she got at me, in her own special way. She wanted to know who the tall man dressed as a burglar had been, but she didn't ask any more. She just kept in my pocket, all the time, and it was brilliant, the way she found a legitimate reason for worrying me. And as if Fate was well and truly against me, Sister Tutor added the weight of her words to those of Home Sister's, with regard to 'looking after Heather', so I was caught. I had to take Heather out with me, too. So I got Sister Tutor's permission to test her on her weak spots.

Heather didn't like this at all. The hand of authority was now against her and she couldn't question me about my life at home any more.

One day she said, 'Ooh, look at that huge chap cleaning the brass on that yacht. Let's go over and look at him! I adore big chaps like that one! Look at his muscles.'

Jeff Watt was stripped to the waist

and his skin was a lovely even tan. He worked rhythmically, and seemed extremely happy in his job. Whether he could see us or not, I had no way of telling. As always, his eyes were covered by dark glasses against the blinding sunshine, and his gesture of finding he had run out of polish seemed perfectly natural to me, but Heather was very angry to see him turn and go below the minute she got near enough to hail him.

I believe she would have gone aboard. There was nothing I could do to stop her. But at that moment Richard walked along towards us and called to her.

She turned and saw us standing together. She let her wide smile slip a bit, as she watched us. Richard said, 'That's my uncle's boat. What are you two doing, going towards it? You weren't intending to board her, were you?'

'Heather wanted to,' I said. There was no point in denying it.

Richard looked nettled. 'Well, tell her to have a bit of sense, for goodness' sake!'

'*You* tell her!' I urged, seeing a way out for just one afternoon. 'Be a dear and take her off my hands. There's something I must do, and I really want to be alone to concentrate.'

'Well, I'd like to,' he said, hesitating, then, obviously deciding it was what he wanted to do above all, he called to her and suggested something. I don't know what it was, but Heather said, 'Oh what will poor Eileen do? She's got nobody to be with?'

'I've got to go to the Post Office,' I said crisply, 'and I really don't want any help. You go off with Richard and think yourself lucky!' So she did, but she kept looking round to see if I'd gone aboard that yacht.

When she saw me cross the road and actually go down the narrow road towards the shops and the Post Office, she eased out and suddenly clung on to Richard's arm.

I wanted to get some money out of my little account, for something new. I was going home at the next free weekend, and Gran worried if I wore the same old things. There had been something said about going to tea at Dr Barclay's, so I drew enough out to buy a plain dress that would answer the purpose, and double up for other occasions, too. It wasn't easy to find something I liked, because my hair looked so awful. I wondered if it might be worth while to get a decent cut and set. It was true what Jeff Watt had said — if I'd gone as an urchin to that Fancy Dress Ball, I might have been a roaring success. Well, I didn't want success based on my normal appearance. I dodged into a hairdressers and was lucky enough to get an appointment right away.

The Boss himself, it appeared. He had just happened to be free and normally wouldn't have taken on a new, and probably casual customer, but he liked a challenge, he said, looking at my hair as if it would be the biggest challenge of his whole career.

He worked on me for the next hour, twittering and bemoaning the way it had been neglected, and thoroughly irritating me.

I said, in what I considered a mild tone, 'Nurses don't get a lot of time to bother about their hair!' which was unfortunate and possibly even silly, for he took me up at once on it, armed with irrefutable evidence to the contrary. He even quoted the glamorous staff nurse of Men's Medical, and one or two young ward sisters, who were all customers of his. I could have pointed out that they had been blessed with glorious silky long hair of a decent colour — two blondes and a redhead, I recalled — and good looks as well, but it hardly seemed worth it.

And he did make a good job of me. He somehow coaxed my hair to — well, not curl. No, that would have been a wild exaggeration. But certainly to cuddle its ends inwards, which gave a neat rounded effect which even pleased me.

I went out into the sunshine so cock-a-hoop, and was blinded by it so that I cannoned straight into a big man who had been striding along, minding his own business — a man whose rather nice yellow cable-stitch sweater looked absolutely gorgeous against his richly tanned skin. He held my arms to steady me and I didn't have to ask myself who he was. The usual riot of excitement tore through me and I could feel my face getting hot. 'Sorry!' I muttered.

'So that's where you rushed off to on your own,' he said, in a low tone, and there was such an odd look in his eyes. His back was to the sun, so I might have been mistaken, but he almost looked tenderly at me! Sorry for me, most like, I lashed at myself, as I remembered all the girls who were after him, and the things I had said about them. Golly, he must think I wanted to join the merry throng! 'It's got to last till next week-end,' I said fiercely, 'because I'm going home to see my grandmother!' and that reminded me that I had left the box with the dress in it, in the cubicle. The girl at the desk came out with it at that moment so I couldn't escape.

Jeff said he'd carry it, and marched me off. 'Where are we going?' I asked.

'To get some tea. I need some. You look as if you do too. And are you going to take that little wretch Heather with you when you go home to your grandmother's?'

'Not if I can help it!' I said, in an unguarded moment. 'Well, I don't think Gran would like a stranger to share our little time together,' I tacked on to that, but it didn't stop him laughing.

'I do like you, Eileen, when you forget to be polite and are just brutally frank.'

I hoped he wouldn't take me to the same place that Richard had taken Heather to. I said so.

Jeff looked so alarmed that he put his dark glasses on again. 'Where have they

110

gone?' he demanded, and then said, 'Never mind, I know a place that they won't. Heavens, we don't want to have a party do we?' and he looked pleased when I said we did not.

Actually I was glad I had made the point, because I didn't suppose he had much money, and it might have made a good excuse to take me down a little lane to a cottage that said 'Teas' and where the little back garden unexpectedly had a view between houses, of the sea. They served up strawberries and cream and Jeff said it was quite cheap, really, and then said, grinning, that the people knew him, and I wasn't to bring along a gaggle of nurses and hope to get a meal on the cheap here.

After the strawberries and cream, there were iced cakes and tea with cream in it. I ate in my own uninhibited way because I don't have to bother about putting on weight, but Jeff just played with a piece of toast, and drank quantities of tea. The woman who served us was the old-fashioned type who called him 'sir', and said she was glad he'd brought along a nice young lady this time, which made him look abashed, fierce, then frankly amused, in that order.

'Is she a nice young lady, do you think?' he asked the little old woman, who considered me, noticed how fiery I could blush, and said firmly, 'Oh, yes, sir, a very nice young lady. You couldn't do better, and if I may take the liberty, I would like to see you stop racketing around and get settled down.'

He said, trying to smile but looking a bit annoyed, I thought, 'Now that's enough, Auntie! Go and get some doughnuts, the ones I like,' but she wasn't in any way put out, and went off chuckling.

'Take no notice of her, Eileen!' he said smoothly. 'She's called Auntie by those who know her, but that gives her no right to tell a chap what he shall or shan't do with his brief spare moments.'

'Or,' I took up crisply, 'to embarrass some idiot nurse who has succumbed to going to tea with you. Is it 'Dutch' by the way?' I finished firmly, getting out my purse.

'No, it isn't,' he said, his smile gone, 'and you should know better, Eileen, the way your grandmother brought you up! When a man asks you to tea, you let him pay, my girl!'

He really was an enigma. I hadn't the heart to tell him that my grandmother would have thought it rather awful of me to accept an expensive tea like this from a man who was employed as the dogsbody of one of the big shots at our hospital. Besides, at times there was something dignified and intimidating about him, which stopped me from saying everything that was in my mind. Caught it off his horrible Boss, I told myself, indignantly.

Still, it was an afternoon to remember with pleasure, the first since I had realized I had lost Richard. For once I wasn't being plagued by Heather nor seeing Richard look yearningly at her, which somehow hurt. But, I reflected,

Gran would have said that Richard was old enough to protect himself from someone like Heather.

Though the women patients were as soppy over Heather as everyone else. She was sent to my ward the next day. They send them over for an hour or two, from the Training School, so that if there is something about the sight of the patients that make them quail, they can be kicked out before too much valuable time is wasted on trying to train them.

Not that Heather minded. She loved it, especially when the old women cried out to her, 'Here's the Golden Butterfly herself, the pretty dear!'

The ward sister even exchanged a smile with them, as she went into her office, leaving me to my temperature round, and Heather to tidy the lockers, a thing she made a pretty pretence of doing.

As I came back, I heard her telling the old ladies something I hadn't heard. 'I don't know where it came from, but it's the most gorgeous thing and I've brought it specially to show you all,' which of course pleased them inordinately. 'Isn't it lovely?' and she brought out a velvet case with what appeared to be a golden butterfly lying in it. 'It's a brooch. Take it out and look at it,' she invited them.

One of the up-patients drifted over to see. I heard one say, 'Here, lass, that's expensive. You can tell by the safety fastener — you don't get that sort of catch on a cheap brooch. I know, because my first husband worked in a big jeweller's shop.'

'Who could it have been?' they all wondered, as Heather took it right round the ward and finished up with proudly showing the ward sister, who advised her rather sharply to have it put in the safe-keeping of the Hospital Secretary, who had a safe in his room. 'You don't want to lose a thing like that!'

Heather said meekly that she would do that, but gave the sister a pitying look as the woman walked away. Sister Markwick was fifty-ish and had probably never had such an expensive piece of jewellery in her life. Heather said softly, 'I expect it's my special boy-friend who sent it, don't you?'

Who *was* her special boy-friend? Richard? Obviously she had meant him, because he told me about it later. 'Eileen, who could have sent her that thing? Good heavens, what made her think *I'd* sent it to her? I haven't got that kind of money! But it must have been someone at the Fancy Dress party!'

'Well, there were a lot of big shots there,' I reminded him. 'And Charley Ross's father is quite well off and he probably has a lot of cash to play with.'

'Not that kind of money,' Richard said, and looked really worried. 'Eileen, are you with her all the time? When she's off hospital premises, I mean?'

I looked at him, considering this. 'Well, no,' I allowed at last, determined to keep it polite. He hadn't noticed my hair cut, though everyone else, even Jeff had, and Heather had been so noisy about it that I wished she hadn't noticed it. 'After all, I have my own life to live, and she's not a child. There's this, too. You look worried about her — '

'I *am* worried about her,' he said in exasperation. 'I've tried to make you see that! But I can't be with her all the time.'

' — and as I was going to say, I don't understand why you should be worried about her or wanting to take such care of her, unless, of course, you're all that keen on her?' I held my breath as I said it.

He didn't look at me as he answered. I don't think he knew the answer. When he did speak, it was to say, 'She's a lovely thing tossed into our lives, yours and mine, Eileen, and by your good nature, she was invited to stay, and I think we owe a duty to her, don't you? She takes my breath away, sometimes, she's so lovely, yet so wilful . . . no, perhaps wilful isn't the word. A child is wilful, but Heather seems to get out of her scrapes, but I sometimes think that one day if we're not careful, she might come to harm.'

'Probably, but if you can't do better than that, Richard, then you won't have convinced me that she's our responsibility, yours and mine. And between ourselves, I don't think she wants to be looked after, or even needs it.'

'I've never known you to be so hard before,' he marvelled.

'No, practical,' I said. 'She isn't a child. She's old enough to start being trained as a nurse. I think she only wanted the roof over her head, and any fun she could get out of it, oh, and possibly to see how nurses and doctors act, for use in any play she's in, in the future, because you know, she really does favour the world of the stage rather than the world of medicine.'

'I think she'll make a good nurse,' he said firmly.

'Oh, then I suppose you're thinking

of marrying her. Well, all doctors should marry nurses, shouldn't they? They are the only ones who will understand and put up with the broken private life.'

'I don't understand you,' he said again. 'You know I can't afford to marry anyone, not until I'm settled in private practice. But that doesn't stop me from admiring someone like Heather, and trying to take care of her.'

'Well, mind she (or other people) doesn't misconstrue,' I warned him, and I was rather annoyed, because he was trying to fool me as well as himself, with all that rot. He would have married Heather like a shot, if she'd been willing to settle down with anyone, I was sure! No, that little wretch was going to have a thumping good time with all of the boys, at least for the present!

Heather confirmed this the next day, when she wanted to see that boat again. It had a morbid fascination for her.

'Look,' I said, 'Richard was rather annoyed about it yesterday — didn't he tell you to keep away from it? His uncle won't like it, and you must know that as well as anyone else! You know his uncle!'

'He's a mean old devil,' she said suddenly. 'He's rude to me. I don't know why he bothered to speak for me. And you're always on about him. You know him! You must do! And you could speak for me — I just want to go aboard and be shown over. That chap cleaning the brass could show us!' and she slewed her head round to look at me.

Oh, no, she wasn't going to have Jeff! I was shocked at myself. What was the matter with me? I didn't always *like* him. I felt it was an odd, not very good friendship. I didn't like the way the touch of his fingers on my flesh could upset me. But with all that, I was, apparently, too possessive about him to let Heather get her little claws in him. I suppose I suddenly saw that she didn't really want people, as such. She just liked the feeling of being able to take men away from other girls, but to put a good face on it, so that people wouldn't think she was doing any such thing. I could have shaken her.

'We are not going near that yacht,' I said firmly. 'As for myself, I have things to do. Chores for some of the patients.'

'All right,' she said meekly. 'What sort of chores?'

She found out soon enough. We went to the poorest part of the town, where the rooms in the little houses were so incredibly tiny that I just don't know how they moved the furniture to clean up.

'Are we supposed to do this?' Heather asked, turning up her nose.

Well, we weren't. It wasn't encouraged at all. They were supposed to ask their relatives or friends to do their shopping, post their letters, look after their homes, but what if they hadn't got any family, and only indifferent neighbours, like these two patients? I could never say no.

We went into the first house, which

didn't belong to the patient but her friend, who had been ill. The patient was fretting for news. Heather didn't like the sight of an ill person in a bed wedged between so many other bits of furniture, we could hardly get to her. But she was pathetically pleased that her friend in hospital had remembered her, and thrilled with our call, seeing new faces, though she was being looked after adequately by her young woman lodger.

That visit wasn't too bad, but the next visit was awful. It wasn't enough that we had to walk through the windy narrow back streets, but this place wasn't even clean. The neighbour who was supposed to be looking after the animals, had children and pets of her own. She had done her best, but you could hardly move, among the rubbishy possessions of a lifetime. It was hopeless. The woman had certainly kept the animals fed, but the cats were old, and the birds didn't help the general stuffy atmosphere. And what was far worse, a very small cage had been overlooked, and the two birds in it had died, and lay on the soiled base.

The woman was horrified. 'Oh, those magazines must have fallen down from that shelf and I missed that cage behind them. Oh, what a mess. What are you going to do with it, nurse?'

I said I was going to clean it out.

'Throw it away!' she and Heather said together, but I couldn't bear to throw out the cage. My old patient would be upset to lose a single thing. So I took it outside and cleaned it up and brought it back. I had left Heather with instructions to tidy the room but she hadn't moved.

The neighbour, anxious to do something to atone, made a cup of tea for us. I made Heather drink it but she didn't like it. The old tabby cat took a dislike to her and kept spitting and growling at her and whined at her until she got up to go. 'He is old and grumpy, but I've never seen him take such a dislike to a stranger before,' the neighbour said, 'especially a pretty young person like your friend here.'

Well, they say animals know!

The neighbour of my patient looked unhappy. 'Such a pretty little thing, too,' she said of Heather. 'And do you mean to tell me that your mother wants you to be a nurse? And do all the horrible things those girls have to do for sick and injured people?' and she clicked her tongue. 'What a waste! You should be somewhere where people can see how pretty you are!'

I didn't feel very happy, then. In fact, I was rather cross with the woman, though she meant well. 'It's what Heather wants to do,' I said crisply. 'Actually she's getting very good at learning the things student nurses have to.'

Heather had an odd look on her face. She was sitting starring at a poster, which had been put in a cheap frame. It looked like a lion-tamer, with the circus background, the sort of thing one cuts from a magazine. The poor old thing who lived here seemed to save lots of things like that, to put in cheap frames. Heather stared and stared, but when the neighbour asked just what she did have to learn Heather was quick enough answering.

'Bones,' she said bitterly. 'The names and shapes and places of every bone in the body, and all the muscles, and glands, and bits and pieces in between, and the vein system.' She turned brooding eyes on the neighbour, who was looking a bit queasy, and she said with sudden enthusiasm, 'Do you know that the heart pumps so many beats to the second and that if you've got heart disease it lurches and thuds and growls and bumps?' and she got up to take the woman's pulse.

'No, thank you, dear. I'd rather not know if my heart's all right or not. It serves me very well, but I'd only worry if you were to find it wasn't going at the right pace. What else do you learn?'

'Hazards to health,' Heather said, with relish. 'Not just smelly drains but houseflies and bugs and fleas and mouldy food and dead birds in cages and old pet animals,' she said, thoughtfully looking at the cat that spat at her. 'We went to the Town Hall yesterday to see how the sanitation department works, and we all got a bath and put on loads of perfume when we got back then we got a rocket for using perfume on hospital premises.'

'Oh, dear. I think you'd better come into my place and have a really nice cup of tea and some cakes,' the poor woman said, no doubt wishing heartily she hadn't started talking to Heather.

'No thank you,' Heather said smartly, 'but I'd like to know if I could get one of those pictures somewhere. Have you got one?' and she pointed to the lion-tamer.

The woman laughed. 'No, I've got something better than a picture. I've got the man himself. Beautiful muscles he's got, hasn't he? I saw you looking at his picture. Antonio Orrivetti, that's his name. He used to lodge here when the circus was in town but of course, Grannie Peters not being here, I said I'd take her lodgers in for her. There's Bianca Piccello, the bareback rider, too.'

Heather wasn't interested in the girl. 'Where can I see this man?' she asked, and the woman told her that he was at the circus at the back of town.

I was glad to leave that narrow little street, and I made myself a promise I wouldn't take Heather with me again. I said, 'What's so special about a lion-tamer's picture?'

'Because I like lions,' Heather said, turning to go the other way, and not listening when I protested, 'Not that way! We're going back to the hospital!' But Heather just kept on, down another back alley, following something I hadn't noticed up till now but which grew steadily louder. The vamping haunting sound of fairground music.

I looked anxiously at my watch. The thing about Heather was that if she wanted to do a thing, it was as if there was some power inside her driving her towards it. It worried me. It was no use trying to talk her out of it. I said helplessly, 'All right, ten minutes more, then we'll really have to go back.'

'If I'm ready,' she said in a preoccupied way. 'If not, you go back. I know you don't like being late, Eileen.' And she sounded so pleasant and reasonable that I was put off my stroke. 'I just want to see him.'

'Well, you won't, you lemon!' I exploded. 'You'll see the circus tents, and the fairground stalls maybe, but the animal show doesn't come on till later. Look, there's a hoarding — let's look at the times,' but she took no notice and went steaming onwards.

She could be the most frightening person at times. I hurried to keep up with her. 'Do you know what?' I said fiercely. 'I'm going straight to Home Sister when we get back, and ask her to be free of you. Some other Second Year can take you on, if you must have a nurse to look after you. But not me! You were really horrid to that poor woman — '

'She was getting at me,' Heather said simply.

'She was not! She was trying to be kind, and all you did was to tell her horrid details about what you learn, which you must know you're not supposed to. It's a rule, not to worry the friends of patients with the gory details.'

'I didn't. I answered her question. You wouldn't have liked it if I didn't. And you can't push me off to someone else, because everybody knows it was through you that I came here.'

I gasped as if I'd had a bucket of cold water thrown over me. 'It was not! You wanted somewhere to go, a job with a roof over your head, and you particularly asked us if we could get you in! You know that's true! And ever since then — ' but Heather broke in, 'Not so! You tell everyone that it was Richard wanting me, and his horrible uncle speaking up for me, when all the time it was you. Why did you? Or do you let every stranger brainwash you into doing something for them?'

'Why, you little horror!' I said furiously.

She burst into tears. Just like that, burying her face in her hands, and coming to an abrupt halt. 'Why do you make me so unhappy? Why are you always getting angry with me?' she sobbed, her voice not particularly quiet.

'I say, do get a hold on yourself,' I begged her. She had stopped outside of one of the caravans, and a man stripped to the waist, in old jeans, was hanging some washing out on a little line. He was such a big handsome important-looking man, it seemed a silly job for him to be doing. And then I recognized him. It was the lion-tamer.

He came over to us. 'What is the matter?' he asked her, with a strong Italian accent. 'Is life treating you bad, yes?'

'Oh, no, not really,' Heather gulped. 'I mean, I must be an awful nuisance, and it isn't every senior who wants to have a junior around, only it all got too much for me. I'll be all right!'

He gave me a very black look. 'The little sister is trouble, no — in my country we love the bambinos!'

'Heather, back to the hospital, or we'll both be late,' I snapped, for this was really beyond everything. I'd just remembered a rule I'd forgotten — we weren't allowed to go to the circus or fairground unless in a party of at least six — one of the antiquated rules of the hospital, but based on a rather unpleasant incident in the past. I took her arm and yanked her along.

She gasped over her shoulder at him, 'Thank you for being kind to me,' as if I and the rest of the world were brutal to her!

'Is nothing!' he shouted. 'Come to Antonio if she's unkind to you any more! *Ciao!*'

'*Arrivederci!*' she said, with a shy smile, and a wave, which brought an ecstatic grin to his face.

I was so angry, I couldn't speak. We

131

left the fairground and got on a bus. It was lucky. We would now just scrape in.

I looked at her, as I bought the tickets. Of course, Heather never thought of paying her share. 'Well?' I said.

She came out from behind her handkerchief, and her face was one big grin. 'Oh, that did me good!' she said, laughing.

I was so astonished, I could only gape at her.

'Sorry I had to paint you in such a black light, Eileen,' she said, briefly gripping my arm in friendliness. 'But I had to do it. I was so *bored*.' She looked straight into my eyes. 'Home Sister said the other day that boredom could be a sickness and it's true. I was so bored, in that horrid little house, that I felt *ill* with it. I had to do something!' She grinned reminiscently. 'I saw that picture and I remembered the circus was in town, and I wondered if I could pull off the old trick again, and I can.'

'You mean you knew him?'

She didn't answer that directly, but said instead, 'I meant I could make a strange man all concerned for me, in less than thirty seconds. Could *you* do that, Eileen?'

'Good heavens, I wouldn't want to!' I said angrily. 'And don't you do it again, or you'll go straight to Matron — I shall see to it!'

She shrugged, as if the point was not worth bothering about. She had done what she set out to. She was no longer bored. She looked almost happy. 'Why don't you leave the hospital and go on the stage? It's what you'd be most good at,' I gritted at her.

She considered me. 'You want to get rid of me, don't you?' She snapped her eyelashes excitedly. She had darkened the lids today and I had only just noticed it. But I couldn't be bothered to tell her to wipe her face clean before she went back to the Nurses' Home. I was suddenly very tired. I had helped young nurses before. It was encouraged in our hospital. In fact, the ward system allotted a student to a Second Year as a habit, when they left the Training School. I briefly prayed I wouldn't get Heather, and wondered how I could get rid of her now. There was this visit to Gran's that I was wanting so much. Surely I wouldn't have to take Heather too?

'No, I neither want you around nor to get rid of you. I'm not all that interested,' I sighed. 'I am just doing this because I have to.' And when she looked patently disappointed, I was absurdly pleased, because I thought that at last I had got the measure of her. Say the opposite to what she wanted: that was all. But I should have known Heather better than that.

I spoke to my grandmother on the telephone that night, and she said straight out that she couldn't do with another nurse that weekend. I could have hugged Gran! And then I paused to wonder why she had been so apparently inhospitable — was she unwell? Anyway, I could now feel armed against the possibility of Heather coming with me. Only one more day to go! Late tomorrow, Friday. I'd be off!

The following day I couldn't find Heather. One of her friends volunteered the information that she had had to go to the Post Office and couldn't wait for me. There were two other students with her, it seemed, so I went off on my own.

There was a strong tide running. People were gathered on the promenade watching the sea smacking up against the knobbly wall, sending sheets of spray high into the air. It was sometimes like this after a storm in the night. The little boats bobbed dangerously. Some of them had been taken away. The yacht club had all their tiny craft pulled up on the wheeled trolleys in such weather. Only the larger boats were left. I went, out of curiosity, to see what had happened to *Seamaid II* and found *Mermaid* in her place. That would please Jeff Watt! I asked a fisherman standing by, what had happened.

'Why, 'tis belonging to one of your top brass at the hospital and he wasn't going to have his boat left there,' the man said with a grin. 'Took her down to the creek, he did.'

'What, all by himself?' I boggled at the thought of that old pathologist, bent over his specimens, snapping at me in that sharp voice, dressed for bad weather on the *Seamaid II*, struggling with the sheets, and taking off smoothly into the teeth of the storm. 'Oh no, he couldn't!' I protested, but the fisherman said mockingly, 'Oh, couldn't he, then? You want to see him, miss! A fine sight to watch, Sir Russington struggling with the canvas in the teeth of a gale! Many's the time — ' but his words were whipped away.

I saw Heather coming along alone. I went towards her, but to my surprise she ran up the gangplank of the *Mermaid* and vanished below. Was it possible she knew the owner? I didn't know whether to follow her or to ask the question I knew I should, before the fisherman took off for shelter. But I had to know.

He spat before telling me. 'Rich American, name of Driscoll. Lawrence Driscoll. Don't know one end of a craft from t'other. Wanted to take her out in this squall. I told 'm — Lor love us, if he isn't casting off!' The man started to run, and so did I. Heather was aboard and it was quite clear that she thought it was the *Seamaid* and, I thought angrily, that Jeff Watt was aboard.

5

Heather had a pink ribbon threaded through her hair and she looked ravishing, in spite of her little nose being pink and her eyes watering. She had a very bad chill and was suffering from shock and had been treated for it, and packed off to the sick bay like any other nurse, but unlike any other nurse, she got V.I.P. treatment, because she had been on board a rich American's sail boat that had come to grief in a storm, and even the press were there.

Honestly, sitting by her bedside (at her special request) I couldn't see how she had achieved it. Any other young nurse in the Training School would have been kicked out for less!

She said again, 'Tell me all over again, Eileen, what happened, after I went downstairs — '

'You mean 'below',' I corrected her

automatically, one eye on the time. I had a train to catch. It was the week-end and I was not going to let anything get in the way of my seeing Gran again. Quite apart from the need to see Gran, I was worried by her lack of hospitality. She *must* be unwell!

'Yes, but tell me,' Heather begged.

I shrugged. She must have heard it three times already, and by all the rules, she should be feeling terrible. But she could still enjoy everyone's anxiety over her, particularly Richard's!

'Well, I jumped aboard as that idiot Driscoll cast off, and the fisherman I was talking to, managed to jump too, but two other chaps didn't and we had to throw them a line.'

'You mean you actually *know* what to do to make a boat go?'

'You don't 'make it go',' I corrected her for the second time. It was no use. Heather, I suddenly realized, didn't want to hear about how we had got the *Mermaid* back to her mooring again, without damaging her too much against the side, in that sea. She didn't care really whether I knew anything about sailing, or whether (as was the case, or almost) that I had simply obeyed to the letter the voice of the old fisherman and the two other chaps from someone else's crew who had come aboard to help us rather than see a fine craft like that, smashed to matchwood against the stone wall. She wanted to hear what had happened to herself.

'What made you go aboard her?' I asked fiercely. 'I suppose you thought it was the *Seamaid II*?'

'Of course I didn't,' she said indignantly. 'Didn't Richard say we weren't to go on to his old meanie uncle's boat? I wanted to know who had given me the brooch and Lawrence Driscoll was the only rich man I knew. I was sure it must be him.'

'And was it?'

'I don't know. I didn't find out. He was making a botch of casting off and then he got seasick and was almost washed overboard, while all the rest of you were screaming things about — pull in that sheet, mind the boom, things like that. What is a 'sheet', by the way?'

I told her mechanically, but I wanted to know something else. 'How did you come to meet Lawrence Driscoll?'

'At the Fancy Dress Party, of course!' she said, her eyes going very wide. 'He was there at the invitation of one of the big shots. Didn't you *know*?'

So that was it. Well, I was glad that Richard hadn't bought that brooch, even though he had already told me he hadn't got that kind of money. 'No, I didn't know, and you'll have some questions to answer, Heather, when you're fit enough,' I said, getting up.

'You're not going?' She was most indignant. 'But I'm ill!'

'And being looked after very well by everyone,' I said, patting her arm. 'But my grandmother isn't well and she is all alone and I must go to her. You'll be fine.'

'But you've got a cold! You can't go

to someone who's not well, Eileen,' she wailed, and that, too, was a point that was worrying me. In spite of Heather's pleas, I slipped away before anybody thought of stopping me. So far the attention had all been on Heather, and nobody had noticed that I hadn't come out of the adventure unscathed. My arm throbbed badly, but I promised myself I'd wait till I got home and ask Richard's father to look at it for me. If I let them see it here, I wouldn't be allowed to go home.

So I was on that train, carrying my week-end case in my one good arm, and wondering dully if I had broken the other or merely got a compound fracture. And when I arrived home, having cadged a lift from the greengrocer driving past our station, I found to my surprise that my grandmother wasn't unwell. In fact, she was in better shape than I was.

'What happened to you, Eileen?' she demanded, coming over to feel my head, and in doing so, seeing the ugly bruise on my forehead. 'Just what is your hospital doing to let you be about in that state?' So I had to tell her.

'It's nothing, Gran. An idiot student nurse got on a boat in a storm and we — a fisherman and I — knew the owner was aboard and was a perfect fool so we — well, we just got aboard, too, and some other people as well, and, well, brought the craft about again. That's all. Oh, this arm? I got thrown against something. The sea was running high. Not to worry.'

'It's that girl called Heather, isn't it?' my grandmother said.

'Oh, well . . . ' I shrugged. Somehow it no longer mattered. 'Oh Gran, I'm so pleased to see you, and so glad you gave me the impression that you weren't well. She wanted me to stay with her and I didn't want to.'

'I didn't mean to give any such impression!' my grandmother said roundly. 'To tell you the truth, girl, I didn't like the sound of her and I made up my mind I wouldn't have her here! Oh, I've heard a lot of nonsense about her from Richard's father. He's worried, too, poor man. Richard has never written such idiotic letters before. Just like a callow youth! Does she want him?'

I shook my head. Gran was already bathing it, with cotton wool in boiled water in a cooking basin and she accidentally touched my arm, which drew interesting sharp noises from me. I couldn't help it. I wasn't ready for it to be touched. It flicked me on the raw. And I was tired and unhappy. 'No, she doesn't want him — not unless she gets the idea that Richard and I have gone back together again, and yes, then she'll want him and get him!' I said savagely.

'Oh. Like that, is it?' she said, thinking. 'And you still as soppy over him as ever, I'll warrant!'

But before I could answer that, a shadow fell right across us where we stood. Someone was at the open door. Gran looked queerly at the person; sort of put out, and worried, and not at all easy. I had to see who this was, but she was preventing me from turning round to see. And then I caught his reflection in a picture on the far wall and a well-remembered voice said easily, 'Hello, Eileen!'

'What are *you* doing here?' I demanded fiercely, and earned a very strange look from my grandmother. I thought perhaps she was on her old hobby-horse — never be rude to visitors. Jeff Watt moved over to me suddenly, and lifted my arm, which made me scream. 'Don't you dare touch it!' I shouted. 'All right, Gran, I'll go to Richard's father and let him fix it, but no-one else, but no-one! Who do you think you are?' I demanded of Jeff, who wasn't taking the slightest notice of what I'd said, but who was gently moving the arm with tender, exploring fingers. 'Leave it! You'll make it a lot worse! What do you think I am — the brass-work on your Boss's boat?'

Gran was shaking her head at me in

an admonishing sort of way. I suppose she didn't approve of any of this. 'Do you know who this is, Gran?' I demanded, suddenly remembering that she might well know Jeff's boss, even if I didn't.

'Of course I do!' she snapped. 'And what happened to the manners I taught you, girl, to everybody?' she retorted.

Jeff said, 'You'd like dear little Richard's Daddy to fix it? Right! I'll take you there, at once, because I think you'll be sorry if it isn't fixed at once!' and before I could say another word, he had, with his usual sardonic grin, swung me up into his arms, the bad arm away from him, and marched me out to where the big gleaming monster of the car belonging to Sir Russington stood.

'Hey, what are you doing with the big car? Won't your Boss want it?' I demanded, slewing round to look up at his face.

He wasn't smiling any more but looking exceedingly grim. 'Now we're out of earshot of your good grand-mother,' he said angrily, 'perhaps you'd tell me how you got into this state and how it was that they let you get away from the hospital without treatment?'

'You tell me first what happened to the *Seamaid II*,' I snapped back, and then to my horror I fainted.

I woke up in Dr Barclay's surgery. I could hear him talking to someone and the water running. My arm felt funny. It had been set in plaster. My head was swimmy and on investigation I found a patch had been put on the bruise. I lay back and considered how I felt: I was not one to get ill, and this was a new thing. I dissected the sensation.

Then what Richard's father and the other person were saying, pierced my consciousness. I don't know how much I'd missed. Richard's father said, 'Well, I don't like it.'

It *sounded* like Jeff Watt answering, but that was silly. He would never dare to say to Dr Barclay, in that scathing tone, 'You don't like it! What about me? And your fool of a son is making things a damned sight worse! Do you realize she's in love with him?'

Dr Barclay sounded really distressed. 'I've thought it for years. They grew up together. I couldn't have hoped for anything better. Frankly, I don't think Richard will ever marry.'

'He certainly won't do anything sensible!' the other voice retorted.

'All very fine for you to talk,' Dr Barclay said. 'You're rising forty and have acquired sense! He's just a boy. All right, all right, so you're thirty-nine. Let's not split hairs. You look younger, so what are you worrying about? And why don't you do something to help the situation?'

'I am, to the best of my ability,' and now I knew it must be Jeff. Nobody else could have that sardonic tone in his voice.

'If that's your best,' Dr Barclay said tartly, 'then let me tell you, that quite apart from what I think about it, Eileen

148

will feel a great deal worse. In fact, I doubt if she'll ever forgive you!'

★ ★ ★

I was shivering and my teeth were chattering. What I had thought at first was a bit of fever because I hadn't bothered to get anything done about my arm and the pain had been building up, now struck me as a definite chill, because, on thinking back, I had only managed to change my top things. My arm hadn't allowed me to skin everything off. Some of my things had dried on me.

I thought, with a sinking heart, that I was going to have a rather disappointing week-end. It would probably be spent in bed.

Gran was furious, of course, and so was Richard's father. But he was a believer in drugs and I was under for some hours and felt a little less terrible when I came to.

With the cessation of the stormy

weather, autumn decided to be bland. There was warm soft golden sunshine streaming in the window of my room in Gran's house, and the winter hangings — dark red and very cosy and warm looking — had been put up. The winter cover of the old sagging beloved armchair — red too — had been stretched on, and the cushions had been re-covered in autumn gold and a cheerful bright yellow. What I could see of them, that is, because a visitor was taking up most of that chair. Jeff Watt.

'What are you doing in my bedroom?' I demanded, but he didn't grin, and it struck me then that he didn't look too well himself and not quite so young and vigorous and sardonic as usual. He reached forward and felt my forehead and said, 'Has anyone ever told you what an idiot you are, Eileen?' Which was a nice matey way of starting a conversation.

And curiously enough I was glad to have him there, though I didn't know why. 'You carried me to the doctor,' I said weakly.

'Why didn't you have that arm seen to at the hospital?' he demanded fiercely. 'And why didn't you get out of your wet clothes — you must know very well what to do! Do you *want* pneumonia?'

'I'm tough,' I said, feeling anything but that. 'Not a tender plant like Heather. Besides, they wouldn't have let me come home to Gran for the week-end.'

'And that was important?' he asked, very gently indeed.

'That came first,' I told him firmly.

'I have heard,' he went on, with that chill back in his tones, 'a most outrageous story of you risking your life to save Heather Maple. Any use begging you to leave her to the faithful males she surrounds herself with?'

'Yes, if you undertake to tell Home Sister and Sister Tutor that I want to give up looking after Heather. Oh, and make Heather understand, too,' I added bitterly.

He nodded. I realized he was taking me quite seriously. 'Oh, Jeff, don't be a mutt,' I begged. 'I can't get out of this. I was on the train with Richard that day — ' and because I felt rotten, weak tears filled my eyes and splashed over on to the pillow. A wet pillow isn't nice and wouldn't have been allowed in hospital, but this was a long way away from the hospital and Gran wasn't in the room to see that I was crying for Richard and the pity of it, because Heather had, without even trying, broken the dream of the whole of my life.

Jeff Watt said, 'Tell me about it, slowly, leaving nothing out, if you feel up to it,' so I did. I can't remember what exactly I said, but afterwards it struck me that I must have given him the impression that it was all on Heather's side and that I still wanted Richard. Jeff looked quietly angry, and got to his feet and stood looking down at me with such a funny look.

'Don't worry, I'll get that silly young

devil back for you,' he said tautly. 'I'll do anything, to stop you looking so wretched,' and he rubbed my head, a little like a big brother would do, but yet not quite like. I didn't understand this at all.

'But how? Why? I mean, why should you try?' I stammered.

He shrugged. 'It was supposed to be quite a different week-end, my dear,' I *thought* he said, but he had his back to me and his voice was low. Then he swung round on me. 'The fact is, you're not as tough as you think you are! And I'm the sort of chap who can't bear a girl being so beastly gallant and getting the losing end of it. Now, you want Richard, so Richard you shall have!' and he stormed out and down the stairs, shaking the little house.

Gran came up with something hot and tasteless and thick, which she said was prescribed and would do me good, and she also demanded, 'What made him go roaring out of my house like that? You?'

'He thinks he can make Richard come back to me,' I said bleakly. 'He's gone to get him.'

'But that isn't what you want, is it?' Gran asked shrewdly.

The tears started flowing again. It was like turning a tap on. I couldn't stop them and I was just crying because I was so miserable. I didn't think I'd ever be happy again. 'No, I don't want Richard — I want *him*!' I choked.

She looked at me. I know Gran pretty well. She is the sort of woman who doesn't say a thing if it's going to hurt or upset someone, but like me, she can't keep her thoughts from her face, and I knew she was thinking that it was too late. I'd lost Jeff Watt.

The week-end turned into a week, two weeks. I was being as petted and spoiled as Heather had been when I left the hospital. But I wasn't happy. I had Dr Barclay dropping in every day, and masses of neighbours and friends dropped in and left me things. Flowers and presents of home-made jam, cakes and things; the vicar's wife brought me hankies she'd embroidered. Miss Larch brought her special baked egg custard. She was the local dressmaker and very hard up but she was good at cooking invalid messes so I ate it to please her. All the warmth of neighbours and friends pressed me towards getting well again and I wondered how I had ever liked going away to the hospital, where life was harsh and raw, a rat-race in itself. That's what weakness after illness does to you.

And Richard came. He leaned over me and put his cheek against mine and said, 'Don't give me a shock again like that, love.' But it was the heart-cry of a brother, not a lover. A man who has almost lost a beloved young sister.

He had to go back every so often for duty, of course, but when I once commented on how much time he was getting off, he laughed ruefully and said, 'It's my uncle! He gave me six of the best, metaphorically, of course, that first day we all heard you'd crocked up

— just as if it had been my fault! He's a rum bird. Would you believe it!'

I was most intrigued. 'Why did he do that?' I asked.

'He said I wanted my head examined and that he'd heard the girl was too good to lose (I could have told him that, anyway) and that I was to take more care of you in future. Well, how the heck can I do that with an independent little monster like you, Eileen? I tried to tell him so but he roared at me — positively roared at me!'

'That can't be good for him,' I said seriously, which for some reason made Richard quietly choke with laughter. When he got over that, he said soberly, 'Honestly, Eileen, my uncle is a pain in the neck. He always has been! Rummest member of my family. It's having brains, you know, and getting to the top. And they're all a bit touched in the Path. Lab. Take old Professor Westfield, for instance!'

I didn't want to. I wanted Richard to

talk about us, and yet I didn't. It was queer. He was here, but it somehow wasn't important. I didn't even think he was in love with Heather any more. He wasn't in love with anyone specially. As I'd always suspected, he was a happy young man, in love with life, and loving all people, everyone. He didn't really hate his uncle: just wanted to keep out of his sight, to avoid trouble.

When I was better, he took me out for drives, and of course, a nurse always itches to get about again, so in the end Dr Barclay had to let me go back to the hospital.

The night before I was due to go, my grandmother came in and sat on my bed. She'd brought up a hot drink for me, and the eternal cup of tea for herself, and sat sipping it and looking at me.

'Say it Gran,' I said. 'You'll explode if you don't.'

'You've changed, Eileen.'

'Well, don't we all,' I said, puzzled.

'No. This is different. I thought (and

so did he!) that it was Richard you wanted. But it isn't, is it?'

I made a discovery. 'Richard isn't like what I always thought he was,' I marvelled. 'You haven't met Heather, but I'd always thought of her as a butterfly sort of person. That costume she wore so successfully suited her so well because that's what she's like.'

'I don't want to hear any more about that girl,' Gran snapped. 'I can't think why you've let her clamp herself on to your shoulders like an Old Man of the Sea.'

'It's her charm, Gran. And when you feel that everyone else likes a person, and know that the charm has brainwashed them, why, one just follows suit.'

'Because you're too weak to make a stand, dislike someone openly because you can see through them and know them for what they are? Is that it?' she demanded.

'No-o, not exactly, because sometimes I am so *for* her that I wondered how I could have felt mean towards her.'

'Yes, I've met people like that before,' she commented.

'And what did you do?' I asked, though I'd guessed the answer.

'Eileen, a person knows in her heart the difference between right and wrong. It's as simple as that. If you feel that girl is wrong, then you shouldn't be blinded by her charm but go right ahead as though it stuck out all over her, what she was like.'

It was no use. Gran wasn't there in Heather's immediate circle. She hadn't even met her, so as it was our last night together, I didn't argue. We talked cosily about other things till she got up to go. And then she said, 'Bless me, I let you talk me round so I forgot to say what I really came up to say! Richard's uncle — Sir Russington! — has taken the trouble to put things right for you,' and she glared at me as she said it. 'He has ordered Richard to stop playing the fool and to get engaged to you.'

'But he can't *do* that! Nobody can!' I gasped. 'Richard doesn't want to become engaged to me!'

'He hasn't said so. He didn't protest to his uncle,' Gran said hardily. 'He asked me last night if I had anything against the idea and I said I hadn't. So he's going to drive you back to the hospital tomorrow, my girl, and don't you play the fool, or you'll have his uncle saying a few things to you!'

'Who does he think he is,' I seethed, 'that he can order people to marry or not, as *he* feels about it?'

'Richard,' Gran observed fairly mildly, 'doesn't seem all that put out. I would have said he was quite willing to marry you.'

I couldn't sleep that night for thinking about it. It was what I had wanted, wasn't it? But did I now? I didn't know. I was haunted by the memory of that man, Jeff Watt, and I kept wondering what *he* would have to say, about his boss shoving in an oar, where Richard and I were concerned.

Perhaps he wouldn't say anything, I concluded miserably. Hadn't he said himself that he'd see to it that Richard came back to me? Perhaps he wouldn't mind that his Boss had got in first. Or perhaps Jeff Watt had been instrumental in seeing to it that the Great Man came down to earth for a few seconds to hear what his nephew was doing to me, and to use his influence on my behalf.

All the same, I wished Jeff Watt hadn't got the wrong idea about it all. Although, I asked myself desperately, what could he have done? His Boss wouldn't have liked it, to find his dogsbody marrying the nurse that his nephew had been brought up with, and whose family were friendly with his, would he? I didn't know. Nothing made sense any more.

Nor did it next morning, when Richard came to pick me up. He tucked me tenderly into the car and we said good-bye to Gran and Dr Barclay and drove off, in the direction of Vicker-sands. But half way there, he pulled off the road in a quiet little backwater, and said, with a lopsided little smile, 'Well, Eileen, it seems I was wrong. I thought you were mad about someone else. But the chap told me no, it's me all the time. So . . . here I am, if you want me!'

6

This should have happened weeks ago, that day on the train when we met Heather. No, just before we met Heather.

Richard's head bent down over mine, his mouth met mine, and the kiss I had longed for, happened. Well, what is a kiss? To analyse it is an insult, and yet, even in the area of my very limited experience, a kiss can be any kind of thing, from the merest butterfly touch of lip to lip, or the hot possession of a mouth resulting in an explosion. Richard's kiss didn't have explosive qualities. It was medium, middle-of-the-way, in every respect. Some day, perhaps, some girl would set him on fire, and he would greedily possess her mouth, but I wasn't that girl. I was glad, in an odd sort of way. There was respect in his eyes, as well as affection, and comfort. He would make a good husband. But he was so self-sufficient. He didn't really need a wife. He had his work. It hung before him like a bright star, leading him on, filling him with satisfaction, in the chase after his goal. And his self-sufficiency left me with a vague, aching yearning that was a little frightening. Was it always going to be like this?

I braced myself to accept it. I had cried for the moon all my life and now I had it, it wasn't like what I had thought it was. Or was it simply that, in modern jargon, I simply wasn't the one who could 'turn Richard on'? I shied away from that, and talked with moderate enthusiasm about our engagement, insisting on a secret one for the moment, and of our marriage — a small intimate affair when he had finished his stint at the hospital, done his time as Medical Officer of Health, and was ready to take over a practice. And all the time, Heather's name wasn't mentioned, but we thought of her.

All my friends were pleased to see me back, anyway, and I slid into my old life as if I had never left it. I had been given another ward. This time Men's Accident. All the faces were new. I had also been given another girl from the Training School, which was a relief. And I made myself a promise that I wouldn't go down the length of the shore where the *Seamaid II* was normally berthed, because I had heard that come hail or high water, that craft at least would be there, even if more sensible men put their sail boats away for the season. And above all, I didn't want to see Jeff Watt.

Heather made it her first call, to see me. 'How are you? What happened to you?' she asked breathlessly, and looked as if she really wanted to know. So I told her, simply, in small words, so she could understand and have no excuse for getting the story wrong.

'I got wet, coming to the rescue of

your Lawrence Driscoll, remember?' I reminded her. 'I didn't take off all my wet things so I got ill. It took a little time to get well.'

'I heard you'd hurt your arm,' she said.

'Yes, that, too. I was flung against the rail, on the *Mermaid*, but I didn't realize it at the time.'

She racked me with hungry eyes. She didn't believe that was all there was to it. 'Have you seen Richard while you were at home?' she asked at last.

'Naturally. His father is our doctor and they are our neighbours!' I was astonished that my voice could sound so casual.

She eased out a bit, but her eyes were now raking my hands so to help her, I did something with a pile of books in front of me so she could see there was no engagement ring, no mark of one. She then looked to see if there was a tape round my neck which would indicate a ring hanging there, and there wasn't.

166

'How have *you* been getting on?' I asked her.

In the past she had been delighted with that question but now she merely looked sullen. 'Oh, so-so. Your beastly friends told me you'd got what you'd always been wanting. What did that mean?'

So that was it! I'd have something to say to them! 'Can't you guess?' I said lightly. 'A long, long week-end with my grandmother, except that I hadn't really wanted to be ill at the time. Still, it was a nice long stretch in the comfort of home. She fussed over me, spoiled me.'

I thought it would set Heather's mind at rest, to know I hadn't been having a wild time with men she didn't know about, but it didn't. She didn't care to know I'd been made a fuss of. 'I wanted to come and see you only Richard wouldn't take me,' she complained.

'How many men have you got on the go at the moment?' I asked.

She shrugged. 'Lawrence Driscoll, of

167

course, but I'm tired of his American accent. And there's that stupid Charles Ross.' She seemed evasive.

'You've got two quite wealthy men there, at any rate, so you should have plenty of treats and outings!' I reminded her.

'Your friends don't like me,' she said, in a tight little voice.

'There's nothing I can do about that!' I said sharply.

'Yes, you can! I want you to! I want you to tell them to stop being horrible to me and glaring at me when they see me.'

'Your friends are hostile to me sometimes,' I reminded her, but of course, she merely shrugged that off, saying, 'That's different. We're the juniors, the under-dogs. We have to stick together.' And after that, she stuck to me like glue, as in the past.

Richard told me on the telephone that he thought one night out a week would be rather nice, and help us to keep our secret. I agreed but wondered helplessly how we could manage it.

Richard, however, had it all settled. 'My dear Eileen, I have no wish for another rocket from my formidable uncle, so I have worked it out. We go out the same night as Heather is taken out by either Driscoll or Ross. Probably Ross. He knows the set-up and will help me. Okay?' and I heard his quiet chuckle at the other end. Had he really got over Heather? I couldn't believe it.

Heather went out the next afternoon and fell into step beside me. 'Where are you going, Eileen?' she asked in a warm, friendly voice, as if we had settled things for this day.

'Just walking,' I said.

'Down where the *Seamaid II* is?' she asked casually.

'Not if I can help it!' I retorted. 'East winds aren't for me, after what I've just had. My grandmother warned me to take care so I shan't go to the shore.'

'All right, then, the circus,' she said, as if it never occurred to her that I was intending to do anything else but be with her.

'Is it the same circus?' I asked idly, but she shook her head. I was distinctly relieved. So we wouldn't run into the lion-tamer.

It was a different circus, on a patch of open ground much nearer the hospital than the last one had been. This was a big, prosperous circus, with glossy motor caravans at the back, for the people travelling with it. Heather said confidingly, 'I want you to do something for me. I've made friends with a girl in this circus. She's a riding act, and she's hurt her back and wants to talk to someone about it. No, don't say send her to the hospital. That's the last thing to do — you lose your job if anyone gets to hear there's a hospital involved. Please, Eileen, just have a look at her for me.'

I was going to refuse. Common-sense reminded me of the trouble Heather had got me into before, by wheedling like this. But she suddenly said, 'Look, there she goes — into that caravan. Come on, let's hurry,' and she took my hand and ran.

The girl had been petite, lithe. There didn't seem to be much wrong with her, the way she swung along. But there was little time to speculate. Heather pushed me up the steps of the caravan and I was in, trying to pierce the gloom. 'Through into the inner room,' Heather whispered, so I went. And then I heard the door bang behind me and a key being turned in the lock. The light snapped on and the girl I had seen faced me.

'What do you want?' she demanded, indignantly. She had half pulled off her jersey, and was holding the spangly garment she would wear on the bare back of the white horse on the posters. I recognized her immediately. She returned the compliment and asked bitterly, 'So where is your little friend? With Antonio again?'

'But you were both in the other circus,' I said, not understanding and tried the door. 'Oh, it's one of her silly tricks!' I fumed. 'Heather, let us out!'

'That is the name!' the girl stormed, putting her jersey on again. 'Well, this time she has gone too far. She comes to see Antonio but today he is practising with Prince who is a very mean lion, and if she goes to him and distracts him they will both be sorry!'

I sat down helplessly. That illness of mine had robbed me of more strength than I knew. 'Oh, don't be silly,' I said. 'Heather doesn't get herself into danger.'

'No, that's just it! Everyone else but not herself!' and the girl's black eyes, under their straight dark brows, were so hostile it was like a blow. 'I tell you, if anything happens to my Antonio through her, I will tell Poppa and then you will all be sorry!'

I wondered many times afterwards, why I had gone with Heather to the circus that day. I suppose I had felt rather secure from her for once, because — whether I wanted it or not

— I was now engaged to Richard, and he would look after me.

The nightmare of that day lives with me still. The girl, who said her name was really Bianca Piccello, and not just a stage name, also said that Heather had known the lion-tamer at some other time and that she was wicked.

I thought at the time that Bianca meant that Heather sort of bewitched him. She hadn't a great command of English but a furious temper. She almost wrecked the caravan, trying to get out.

Finally we had to climb through one of the windows after she had broken it. The glass caught my arm and blood flowed freely. Absently I wound a clean hankie round it, and then I slipped getting to the ground. Bianca was already running.

People were about but all minding their own business. There was a man with a string of baby elephants, and one with some chimps. Bianca shouted something at the elephant man, who shouted to someone else and started to get his animals back before he ran to help her. But it took time to put the animals back and we, in the end, reached the place where Antonio was with his lions.

It was the big handsome man with the muscles, who had spoken to us at that other circus. I remembered him. He was surrounded by lions. This circus was evidently trying to be different. None of the dreary old acts I remembered from childhood. I stood still and watched Antonio getting his beasts up one after the other, on to a see-saw, from which they jumped each other through a hoop of flames. Cold fire, I believe it's called, but it looked real enough to me.

As they leapt through the hoop they were catapulted through another hoop covered with paper. The first lion — the big one — had to break it open. It was at a different level, and this beast obviously didn't like doing it. But Antonio got him up, and the others followed. While the big truculent one was kept moving, doing his part of the act, the others were all right. They even followed him through a sort of big drainpipe and up on to another seesaw to the jumping routine again.

But Heather was outside the cage, watching, and I could see she was distracting Antonio. He kept glancing at her.

Somewhere I had read that so long as you could concentrate, hold the gaze of a wild beast, you could make it obey. Well, Heather wasn't letting him do that.

Sweat was pouring down his face, and his small store of English had gone. He was shouting in Italian at the beasts, and in that language to Heather to go away. It didn't need a knowledge of the language to know what he meant. But she didn't move.

And then the big lion wouldn't go through. He paused at the top and the others stopped, undecided. Antonio cracked his whip at them but without the movement of the leader they could do nothing right, and one by one they jumped to the ground and two started fighting.

Heather gasped, 'Look out, Antonio, he's going to jump you!'

Bianca screamed at her to come away; the men closed in. Then Heather, who was about the only one in all that throng who didn't understand that Antonio's command in Italian meant stand perfectly still and quiet, shouted, 'I'll come in the cage with you — take their minds off you!' and she ran towards the cage door.

Someone stopped her, of course, just in time, but the damage was done. Antonio was doing a wonderful job of getting all the other lions back in their places, but he had lost his grip of the big one. You could see the triumph in the very set of the beast's head, as it ignored his whip and jumped him.

Heather just stood there, frozen, her hands clapped to her face, her eyes enormous, while everyone else ran. I didn't see what they could do, but one of the men got the other lions moving up the tunnel and back to their quarters, and two others used a net to get the big one, while Antonio rolled away. He had been clawed badly.

I knelt by Antonio, doing what I could, till our own ambulance came. I think it must have been out cruising, it was there so quickly. And all the time I kept remembering that split second, before the big lion jumped Antonio, and I kept seeing Jeff Watt in that position, and I couldn't help thinking that I might just have done what Heather had done: threatened to go in with him and help. Except that I shouldn't have been such an idiot as to stand and watch him and distract him, in the first place. Also, if it had been someone like Jeff Watt, he wouldn't have allowed any girl-friend of his within miles of him at such a time, and what Jeff Watt ordered, would have been obeyed.

Antonio wasn't blaming Heather. She

was near him now I had got all his wounds covered with stuff from the First Aid Box that someone had shoved at me. She was crying, and quite sincere about it, I knew. He whispered, 'Cara mia,' and begged her, 'Don't cry!' and then he couldn't say any more, because he was in such pain. The girl Bianca was standing behind Heather. Antonio didn't even look at her as they carried him out on a stretcher.

I couldn't look at Bianca. Her grief and agony was too naked and her hatred of Heather was building up, too.

'Best take your friend away, miss,' one of the men muttered. So I took Heather in a taxi. My arm was bleeding pretty badly and I held it to me. Heather didn't notice it. She sobbed on my shoulder.

'He's hurt and I did it,' she kept saying. But I hadn't got it in me to tell her that it hadn't been her fault. It had, and she knew it, too.

'What will happen?' she sniffed, mopping her face.

'To him, or to you?' I asked her carefully.

'To me.' She sounded surprised that I should think she meant anything else. Something snapped inside me.

'You really are a selfish little pig, Heather!' I burst out. 'You must know very well that it's asking for trouble to go and distract a man while he's working on something like that! Besides, it's his living! Why don't you have a bit of sense and grow up?'

She shrank before my attack, but she answered, quietly enough, 'I was there by his invitation. He said it would be all right to go and watch him working with the big cats. He said so!'

'Well, you must have known he was being over-confident. Why did you go anyway?' I gasped. 'You must know it isn't allowed!'

'But it's all right while I'm with you,' she pointed out. 'You are so well in with the Barclay family and Sir Russington is the Big Shot there, so it will be all right. I won't get into trouble.'

'You — are — the — end!' I said, on a low note. 'In the first place, Matron is still the boss where the nurses are concerned and in the second place, I can't see Sir Russington bending any rules to suit someone as unimportant as me! Can you?'

'Yes, of course!' she said simply.

I couldn't decide if she was getting at me or whether she was more stupid than even I thought she could be. I snapped, 'Well, he won't, and if he did, I wouldn't have it. And I'm going to see Matron about you, the minute I get back.'

'What will you tell her?' she asked, softly. 'I mean, you did agree to go with me. And you did leave me all by myself, while you went to talk to that girl in the caravan, didn't you?'

'But you insisted that I should go and see her for you,' I began hotly. 'Besides, you locked me in!' Then I stopped.

Heather was looking at me with a bland look in those bright eyes of hers. She would deny locking me in. If

Bianca backed me up, Heather would say she was bound to do so, because she was a rival for the lion-tamer's favours. No-one would believe that anyone like Heather would do such an imbecilic thing as to lock me in the other girl's caravan with her.

And to Heather's way of thinking, this was all quite fair. We were a lot of girls together, and if one could get above another by sheer trickery, that was all in the game. I could only be very grateful in my heart that Richard was now engaged to me, even if I hadn't had it made official with a ring. If he had gone on pursuing Heather, she would have ruined him, for Richard's rules were like my own: we played fair, both of us. And she didn't.

* * *

I was quite certain that Heather would be asked to go, after that incident. But she wasn't.

Frances and I talked it over. 'Who

gave her that expensive brooch? Did you ever find out, Eileen?' she asked.

When I said no, she said, 'Well, I think someone gave it to her to make her think she'd got a rich admirer, but I think it was just someone we know.'

'Well, who, for instance, and why would anyone give her something so expensive just to make her think someone else had done it?' I protested scathingly.

'I don't know,' Frances allowed. 'Does she know about you and a certain person you're seen about with and which we know we mustn't mention his name?' she asked delicately.

I stared at her in sheer surprise. Was it possible that she and the others had found out about our secret engagement, Richard's and mine? The one arranged so forcefully by his terrible uncle? I said, 'Oh, no, I hope not! Oh, no! Oh, Frances, she couldn't, could she?'

Frances said, 'I wish I knew, Eileen.

You really do care for him, don't you, even though you pretend otherwise?'

I blinked. I thought I had worn my heart on my sleeve for long enough, about Richard. But then, of course, since I'd thought I'd lost him, I had gone out of my way to avoid him. Perhaps that was what she meant. I said, 'I just don't want anyone to know about it or to talk about it or stare at us when we're together. I want to protect it, from people like Heather. You know what I mean?'

Frances nodded vigorously. 'Oh, yes, do I not! And I'd feel the same. I think you've been pretty clever about it, too, only I know you so well, that I guessed. Eileen, I do hope it will go all right for you. I mean, well, I'd like you to have everything, and someone like him for life, well, I think a girl like you deserves him!'

'That's very sweet of you, Frances!' I said, in what sounded to me like a hollow voice. It was too late, all much too late. It wasn't Richard I wanted now. He was a sweet person, very kind and he would make a wonderful husband, but my heart was being torn out of me for someone else. And because she was looking so oddly at me, I was afraid she would guess, so I said, 'It isn't always nice, though, being soppy about someone, not when it's the real thing.'

'No, I know that,' she agreed.

'I feel rather sick sometimes, and sometimes I think there's more agony to it than pleasure,' I went on wretchedly, and she agreed about that, too.

'And you don't want someone like our little friend guessing and sticking her little oar in, either,' Frances said warmly. 'And while we're on about her, do you think she's just playing about with the lion-tamer or is she really soppy about him?'

The idea was ludicrous. 'Of course not!' I said. 'What a silly idea! What made you say that?'

'Well — ' she said, expressively,

spreading her hands wide.

'Oh, if you mean why did she go and do what she did, I think she's just enjoying making a play for him because she knows that Bianca, the bareback rider, is that way about him. She just wants to take him away from his own girl. Isn't that her all over?'

'You know she's sitting by his bed, don't you?' Frances said.

Other hospitals might be up to the minute, with their special care units, and a nurse at a big instrument board watching the progress of four or five patients being electronically recorded, but not our hospital. Oh, no, we still did the old-fashioned 'special'-ing system. Apart from other things like finance and space, the powers-that-be considered it a better way to have an individual nurse on duty by the side of a sick patient. Individual care. But why Heather, who was irresponsible and had caused the trouble in the first place? It was beyond me.

Frances went on, 'She's doing very

well at the job, from what I hear. I find her a bit sinister, if you want to know. If I could write her off as a pest, or a spoilt brat or any other label we know and understand, I'd feel better. But half the time I am wondering just what she is really like underneath, because she isn't all bad, and not all inefficient or imbelic. Besides, I often feel I want to kick her and then she goes and does something that makes me feel an absolute beast.'

'Me, too,' I said gloomily. That had been the effect she had had on me from the start. Putting me on the wrong foot all the way.

* * *

I got a sight of Heather the next day, sitting beside the lion-tamer. He was a very strong man, but even the strongest can't go through what he went through for nothing. He lay very quietly, and looked rather odd, such a funny colour. I had only seen him looking hale and hearty, dark-skinned and glowing with health. I had the odd sensation that Heather had done to him what she had done to the rest of us: sapped the strength from the person, in a kind of mental challenge. She had to bend people her way, and if they got hurt, it didn't matter.

When she came off duty for lunch I spoke to her. 'Did you know that he and that nice Bianca person were going to be married?' I had to ask her. I had to know. I prayed that she hadn't really known that.

Heather frowned. 'Aren't you going to ask me how I'm standing up to seeing him so ill? I love him, you know. I can't bear it that he's so ill!'

'He isn't yours to love,' I told her fiercely. I think it was the first time I had ever got really savage with her but I couldn't get out of my mind the look in that other girl's eyes. I kept thinking what a dreadful way it was to get a living, working with wild animals to make entertainment for other people.

Practising every day. Dancing on the bare back of a horse and leaping through obstacles and having to land safely on the horse's back as it came underneath. Things like that, just for a living; things taking iron nerve and precision and skill, and eternally practising, while someone like Heather comes along and treated your lives as a child might treat a pretty new toy. Heather didn't even *feel* what she had done to those people. Just for the moment she wanted the lion-tamer.

She said, 'All's fair in love, don't they say?' which stung me to retort, 'And what would you do if you knew that Richard had found someone? Drop the lion-tamer to go back and take Richard from his new girl? What a busy life you must lead!'

She looked all kind and good. I don't know how she managed it but she did. 'You're just sore, Eileen, because Richard won't fall in love with you, that's what it is. You see, you don't take enough trouble with your appearance, you know. Let's get out, when I'm off duty, and see if we can fix you up to look nice for the October Hop. They've been telling me about it. It's best bib and tucker, I believe.'

I looked at her unbelieving. 'How can you bear to talk about a dance when someone you care for is lying so ill?' I exploded.

'They say you're going to be a good nurse,' she mused, 'but I don't think you'll ever make a nurse because you get all fussed about things that don't matter. Look at me! All the people belonging to me who have died — if I got all fussed about it, I'd be a wreck! Oh, I'm sorry about them, let's be honest. I've got *over* missing them. Life has to go on, so I keep myself interested in something all the time — '

'Yes, other girls' men,' I said bitterly and turned away.

She fell into step beside me. 'And another thing,' she said. 'I never fall out with people. It's a bad thing. I don't care how cross you get with me, I shall never dislike you for it, Eileen. Because I liked you from the start and I mean to keep it that way.'

That was the trouble with her, you just couldn't throw her off, no matter how she sickened you. I said nothing, but she kept on talking. 'Come and have a bite with me and then we'll go out,' she suggested warmly. 'There's another nurse taking over by poor Antonio's side. He said he wants me to go out and get fresh air and go on living. His policy is just the same as mine. Life must go on. We're two of a kind.'

I said nothing, and thought hard about Jeff Watt, and wondered why he was keeping out of my way. Could it have leaked out about me being secretly engaged to Richard? I could just imagine his cynical grin, if he did find out about that. I wished the aching yearning would go. It wasn't sense to keep wanting that man. What would Richard and his terrible uncle say, if they ever discovered?

Heather went on, 'You know, if I didn't know you better, I'd think you were in love. You're not really, are you, Eileen?'

'No, I am not,' I said firmly. Even stupid me knew the danger of letting Heather stumble on such a thing!

'I used to think you walked along the shore where the *Seamaid II* was sometimes berthed, for a special reason. Wanting to see somebody, I mean,' she went on. And as I still didn't answer, she pressed, 'You would tell me if *you* got someone, wouldn't you? You know all about *my* friends.'

I had to steer her off. There was a little sore place in my heart where the memories of Jeff Watt were hidden, and I couldn't have her turning them over, probing them, exposing them to the light, not for anything. I said, 'Have you discovered yet who gave you that highly expensive brooch that you were showing people round the ward? Was it Lawrence Driscoll after all?'

'Oh, him! No! Besides, I'm tired of

him. That man is just a rich bore. Goodness, I like money but not all that much!' she said virtuously.

'So what will you do about it?' I insisted.

'Just wait and see,' she said serenely. 'A man doesn't give a girl a present like that, without turning up for payment.'

'What a rotten way of looking at it!' I exploded.

'No, a sensible way,' she explained kindly. 'In this life you don't get things for nothing. I'm glad I'm me, and not a dreamer like you, Eileen. You don't live, you just dream of a handsome hero coming along. And while you dream, a realist like me comes along and snaps him up from under your nose.'

7

Gran wrote me a long letter next day. I wasn't expecting one from her and she kept on about who was I going around with when Richard was on duty, and not to just keep indoors until Richard was free because he wouldn't want that, and Richard would like me to have other friends as well. And if I found it was someone else I cared about and not Richard, better say so now, before too many people got hurt. It was a very queer letter, coming from Gran. She also said that she hoped I wasn't giving too much time to that tiresome girl Richard had told her we'd met on the train. Funny, without ever seeing Heather, Gran had taken an instant dislike to her.

I was going to show Richard that letter, but in the end I didn't. It was his day off and he told me on the telephone that he wanted me to meet him outside the main gate, and the exact time, and warned me not to keep him waiting. That wasn't like Richard, either, especially as the time he had fixed was just when Heather would be safely at her classes.

I wondered a little about him. He never lost his kind look, his air of loving everyone, and yet he must have seen through Heather for he didn't rush around after her and defend her any more. Or was it just that he was keenly aware that his uncle would be keeping an eye on him?

I was so bothered about that aspect of it that I made up my mind to ask Richard outright all the things I wanted to know about that uncle of his. It struck me that if the man was so influential in Richard's life that he could make Richard stop running around after Heather and promise to marry me, what sort of a life would we have at his hands after I had married Richard? Dancing to the tune of some elderly Big Shot wasn't my idea of a carefree happy married life.

Richard had said we were to have a lazy day by the sea, and a meal in a smart hotel in the evening. Although it was autumn the weather was bland, the hazy gold sunshine almost persuading us it was still summer. Warm, but the night would be chilly, so I took the fluffy imitation fur jacket I had bought two years ago and wouldn't give up because it wasn't expensive fur and I didn't have to worry about leaving it behind somewhere. Gran hadn't liked it and Richard wasn't going to care for it. I could see that, the way he looked at it as I slung it over one shoulder. He, as usual, looked impeccable, neat and gorgeous, but he didn't stir me one bit, and I was bewildered, and vaguely unhappy about it. What was I doing, pursuing an old love like this, just because his uncle had said it was to be so?

With that in mind, I refused to get in

the car though Richard stood impatiently holding the door open. I think he was afraid that Heather would make an excuse to leave her class and run out and ask to come too. I said, 'Richard, about your uncle — '

'*What* about him, love?' he asked wearily. 'Do get in the car.'

I stood my ground. 'If you don't answer my question now, I don't think I'm going out with you today — you evade it every time.'

'*What* question, Eileen?'

'Well, for a start, I don't even know what he looks like!' I burst out, in exasperation.

It was silly to stand there arguing. There were too many people about. Richard's day off was a hospital day for everyone else and I should have known better than to be apparently conducting an argument in full view of everyone else. Richard flushed, and said in a nettled tone, 'If you want to know all that badly, take a good look over there,' and he pointed back at the hospital.

'There he goes!'

I was so eager to see him that I rushed back through the gates but there were so many people about and I was distracted by the sight of Jeff Watt, hurrying over to the car park. It was like a tidal wave rushing over me. I stood there, shaking a little, shocked beyond words that the sight of Richard's uncle's manservant could reduce me to such a state. I wanted him, as I had never wanted any other man. It was awful. I wanted him to be in the car with me for the day, and not Richard. I wanted him to take me into those strong arms and to bring his dark, maliciously smiling face down to mine, and to kiss me. The mere thought of it left me weak and shaking, and sick and ashamed that I should be thinking that about another man, when there was Richard waiting to be my escort for today, my escort for life!

What, I thought, would that man think if he knew what I was thinking as I watched him striding along, his muscular body movements beautiful to watch? He had probably forgotten my very existence, I jeered at myself. He looked neither to right nor to left, but purposefully ploughed through the knots of people, obviously concerned only with getting the great man's car out in a hurry. Perhaps he'd been given a rocket, just like the rest of us.

I closed my eyes and did my best to feel normal again before turning to Richard, and then I remembered what I was supposed to be looking at. His uncle! 'Where?' I asked stupidly, but Richard merely shrugged and said, 'Didn't you see him? He's gone now. He doesn't hang around, and I wish you wouldn't. Do come on!'

I got in the car without further argument, scared that he would notice how upset I was and want to know why. We were well beyond the town and in open country, before I said anything, and then my voice didn't sound quite right. 'Did he look cross?' I asked.

Richard shrugged. 'I take it you're

still talking about my uncle, though I can't think why. He looked much the same as usual. Eileen, know what I thought we'd do today? Buy the rings.'

If he'd wanted to put my mind neatly on another subject, that certainly was the way to do it. For a moment I couldn't think what he was talking about. 'The rings?' I echoed stupidly.

'Yes,' he said, and laughed. 'At the risk of making you in a boiling temper again, my dear uncle suggested that I do it without further delay. Not just the engagement ring but the wedding ring, too. And he wants us to get married quietly and quickly. Suits me. How about you?'

It didn't. Everything in me screamed out against such a thing, and yet not so long ago I had been eating my heart out for something like this to happen. I said, 'Do we have to? I mean, what's the rush? What's it to do with him, anyway?'

'I don't know, to be honest,' Richard said frankly. 'You know me, love. We've been friends all our lives, you and I. I confess I wasn't looking for marriage yet. Too much to consider about stabilizing one's position. Only it is a bit different, you must admit, when the one rich chap in the family kindly suggests fitting a chap out with whatever he needs (a practice in my case) only my dear uncle did rather hope I'd take over a private clinic he's interested in, in Switzerland. So as he's providing the future, financially, I suppose we must fall in with his idea of time and all that. Don't you? What do you feel about it, love?'

I thought about it. If we were to go to some other country after we were married, perhaps I could forget Jeff. Perhaps my old devotion for Richard would come back. After all, it was the stuff that made a good marriage; good steady life-long devotion, not the heady stuff of my feeling for Jeff, which made me almost feel like fainting on the spot. How long would that sort of feeling last? And how did I know what

Jeff felt about me?

Oh, it was all so confusing. I gave it a lot of thought and tried to sort it out in my mind.

Richard said, 'Something you don't like about it, love?' but he sounded well pleased.

'I shall be such a long way from Gran!' I protested, but Richard said sweepingly, 'Oh, stuff, we can send for her to come and stay with us.'

'She might not like travelling.'

'Well,' he said slowly, 'part of the bargain is that we don't come back, and I don't see how we can, really. It's not a job I can keep leaving. I shall be in charge.'

I didn't like it, but of course, it fitted. The autocratic old gentleman probably liked fixing people's lives. 'Is it what you want, Richard?' I asked him, and he said easily, 'Of course! I'd be an idiot if I didn't take a chance like it. Anyone would. Don't you agree, love?'

'I somehow thought of you as working your own way up, in towns and villages in this country.'

He thought about it. 'Like, for instance, Dad,' he mused. 'Working hard all his life, because he likes that sort of thing. I don't know that I'd want that. What I really wanted, to be honest, was research, but I suppose I'd never have the nerve, since it's my uncle's special thing. One doesn't copy the great man in one's family. I wonder if he knows that, and he wants me to — Oh, no, I wouldn't suspect him of anything so unworthy,' he said, half to himself.

'Why, you like him!' I exclaimed.

'Did I ever say I didn't?' Richard countered, in surprise.

We discussed it when we reached the coast and had parked the car. We walked along the edge of the sand together. It was hard and wet-looking. The tide had only just gone out and had left ripples in the sand, and little crabs and things were still crawling about in surprise at the unexpected bright sunshine above them instead of the green, gently lapping water. I couldn't think straight. I said, because I knew we had to sort this out today, before those rings were bought, 'There's so much about it that I don't understand, Richard. I loved you all my life — '

'Yes, I know, love, and somehow the uncle got wind of it, too, though how, I can't think, as you don't seem to know him!'

It was something that puzzled me, too. I said, 'I don't think I like someone else arranging my life for me. I mean, if you'd said to me, that day on the train (the day we met Heather) that you wanted to marry me, well, I'd have been in Seventh Heaven!'

He looked seriously into my eyes. 'I had intended to say just that, only we did meet Heather,' he said slowly. 'And she did rather put every other thought out of my mind. I don't mean,' he hastened to clarify, as I shot up my head indignantly, 'that I fell in love with her. Not that at all! No, it's a quality she's got, of commandeering the thoughts and energy of everyone around her, and of making people feel responsible for her, so that one can't give full attention to one's own affairs. One tends to put them off until after Heather's situation is settled . . . but it never seems to get settled. It goes on and on, and one wonders when one will be free to pursue one's own life.'

'Yes, I felt like that, too,' I admitted, and I kept on thinking of that particular day, and if that had happened — Richard and me — I would never have met Jeff Watt and fallen desperately in love with him because I had only gone down to that end of the shore in deep dejection and desperation, and because I wanted to get away from everyone I knew.

Richard stopped and took me by the shoulders. 'I get the feeling, love, that you and I were meant for each other up till that day when we met Heather, and then something happened. Something slipped out of line, and nothing's been the same since, and I don't see how we can make it the same ever again. Do you feel like that?'

'I just don't know, Richard,' I said miserably. 'I just don't understand it at all.'

'Me, too, love,' he said on a low note, and he pulled me to him so that my face rested against his shoulder, and I could feel his chin on the top of my head. 'How will you feel, married to me?'

I ought to have been able to say, with my heart in my voice, 'Super!' or some such thing, and to really look as if I meant it. But all I could manage was, 'I think you'll make a good kind husband, Richard.'

He looked deep into my eyes. I said, because I felt I ought to say it, 'How will you feel about being married to me?'

He surprised me by saying, 'I always thought of that as the way my life would go, but now, well, to be honest, there are times when I feel that though you're looking at me, you're thinking of someone else. Look at you now! Colouring to the roots of your hair! Eileen, for heaven's sake, if you've met someone else, say so. Don't let's get married with some other chap's shadow between us!'

'Oh, Richard,' I said brokenly, and I couldn't meet his eyes. 'He doesn't know it. He's got no idea. And anyway, as it happened so quickly, it can't be the real thing, can it? It must be infatuation or something silly, that I'll get over, won't it?'

'I don't know, my dear,' he said. 'Who is this chap? Do I know him?'

I couldn't, no matter how I tried, tell him that it was his uncle's manservant. That I had been looking at that man today and so missed seeing Richard's uncle who was being pointed out to me. I just couldn't. So I just mumbled, 'Jeff Watt. You don't know him,' and I hoped that Richard wouldn't know his name, though it didn't seem very likely. I remembered Gran's letter at that point, but before I could frame the words to tell him about it, he swung the initiative away from me. He tilted my chin. 'Eileen, I believe you're pulling my leg!' he said unaccountably, and he was grinning broadly. 'Kiss me, love and let's see if a lifelong devotion has gone for a Burton overnight,' and he put his mouth down on mine and claimed it.

He'd never kissed me like that before. I'd dreamed about it, often enough, in the past. I'd lost sleep over it, too. I'd wanted so badly to be kissed like that by Richard, to be the one thing in his life that mattered. But now it was so much emptiness, ashes. How could it be so, my heart clamoured? And if this had happened to my so-called love for Richard, how could I be sure that any love I might have for another man, would be any different? Jeff Watt, for instance?

I closed my eyes and thought about him, and because Richard had looked so bothered about the way the kiss had turned out, I threw my arms round his neck, and I did try to put something in that new kiss, but I was thinking of Jeff, and the spark was there, and for a moment I felt I was kissing Jeff, until I couldn't bear it, and I pushed Richard away, my face hot and my eyes smarting. I would cry, if I wasn't careful.

But Richard couldn't be expected to understand what had happened, so of course that second kiss satisfied him. 'There you are, you see?' he murmured, throwing an arm round my shoulders and starting to walk with me in the matiest fashion. 'You know what?' he continued, thinking. 'You always were shy about . . . things, Eileen. I should think you'll be all right when we *are* married, and we can go away and start in a fresh country and not have any worries about money, or people like Heather, for instance. How does that make you feel?'

I nodded, because it was all settled really, wasn't it, by his uncle. Perhaps his uncle wouldn't do anything else for Richard if this marriage didn't come off. There was that to think of!

And besides, I'd known Richard all my life. Who safer for a husband? But what did I know about his uncle's manservant, except that he could look at me in a certain way and arouse me to a raving anger, and he could look at me in another way and make my bones seem as if they were about to melt. When he looked at me like that, I forgot everything I believed in or had ever wanted. I was a stranger to myself, a stranger with a hungry yearning that made me sick and ashamed, and alarmed, too.

No, better settle for Richard, I told myself, and then I told him, firmly. 'I would like us to buy the rings, Richard, and get it over with,' was what I actually said. And it didn't sound very encouraging.

Richard laughed a little. 'We'll look at some rings. You can make your mind up some other day. For some reason you're upset today and I for one am not going to rush you.'

'What about your uncle?'

He hesitated. 'He isn't an ogre, you know, Eileen. If I've given you that impression, I must have been rather annoyed over something or someone — perhaps Heather. I don't know. No, my uncle is a very good man. He hasn't had a very happy life, poor chap. Tends to keep to himself. When any of us wants financial help, he's there, at the double. He just begs us not to want him to be social, that's all.'

'How old is he?' I asked, thinking of the crouching figure in the shadows of the Path. Lab.

'Do you know, I'm dashed if I know how old he really is, and if you want me to ask him I can tell you outright I wouldn't dare,' Richard laughed, so I let it go.

We walked back along the edge of the water, curiously lighter in heart, and we enjoyed our day together. We went to a very expensive jewellers (which I protested about, ineffectually) and we looked at rings. Richard wanted conventional diamonds. I wanted anything but the conventional thing, so we wouldn't have agreed, anyway.

As for choosing a wedding ring, I said I didn't want to. I was superstitious about it. I let him take my size and I said he was to get a ring for me and present it on the day, my wedding day.

It had been a very pleasant day indeed, a day in which we had drawn together again, Richard and I, so that we were as we had been before Heather came. He talked to me about the patients, people on the staff, and his dreams for the future, which weren't over-ambitious, after all. He was a dedicated doctor, only happy when he was working. He liked people, honestly liked them, no matter what they were like, so perhaps it wasn't so surprising that he had reacted to Heather in that way.

As for me, I told him of odd funny things that happened on my new ward.

Being me, funny things did tend to happen. It was nice, comfortable, hearing Richard chuckle, and put in the odd comment about the ward sister, or the consultant and his 'firm' who had featured in my stories. It was comfortable. But not romantic.

As Richard put me in the car to return to the hospital, I took myself to task on that score. How could it be romantic? We had known each other all our lives; one thing we could never have that other couples could, was that delicious finding out about each other. We — Richard and I — knew too well what the other person liked and disliked. We knew, too, about each other's families and family history; where we had spent our holidays over the years, where we had been educated and how. So what was left? Was that, I asked myself, how it always was when next-door boy and girl romances gentled themselves into marriage? No excitement? It couldn't be true!

Well, of course it couldn't, I suddenly

realized. They might know all about each other, but then they would have a new finding-out, with the sunburst of passion, the discovery that each 'turned each other on'. I didn't turn Richard on. He didn't turn me on. No, it took someone like Jeff Watt to do that.

Richard talked lazily as he drove, apparently unaware or untroubled by the fact that I didn't bother to answer. I was caught up with the shocking realization that all my married life with Richard would be bedevilled with the what-might-have-been, every time I remembered Jeff Watt.

As if to push this home, something happened to destroy that day. As we slowed to turn into the gates of the hospital, a car was approaching to come out. It was Sir Russington's sleek dark limousine, with Jeff at the wheel; Jeff looking super in a well-cut dark lounge suit, his white collar gleaming against the darkness of that tanned outdoor skin of his. His head was flung back, concentration in his face, as he looked for oncoming traffic. Beside him, looking very much like the cat that has got the canary, sat Heather Maple.

8

Richard saw them, too. He ever so slightly twitched the wheel, in sheer surprise, I suppose. He glanced at me, and caught me staring over my shoulder, squinting to get a last look at them as the big car went out of the gates past us. 'High flyer, isn't she?' Richard murmured, with a low-pitched whistle, but he looked fussed, I thought, in spite of what I thought of as a sardonic comment.

Words failed me. 'Well! And she's supposed to be crazy about that poor lion-tamer! She's got him away from his girl-friend!'

Richard's expression was comic. 'Is that a fact? She's 'gone on' the circus chappie? Lumme!' He was thinking of Jeff, I could see. 'I say, wonder if *he* knows that? I must say I never saw him in the old imagination as having

215

to be in open competition with a lion-tamer! Dare I see that he does know about it?'

I couldn't understand Richard. He wasn't one to perpetrate silly jokes like that. I said, 'Good gracious, leave it alone, Richard! It's not worth even noticing!' I told him crushingly, and besides, I didn't want his uncle to start getting annoyed at what his driver did with the car and someone like Heather. 'Let's forget we saw it,' I added, and I sat there hating Heather with every fibre of my being.

Richard said, with something like relief in his tones, 'You think we should do that? Yes, I'm sure you're right, love. What a pet you are! You're so good to everybody. I'm terribly fond of you, you know, Eileen! You do realize that, don't you?'

He looked so anxious, poor lad, and I couldn't think why. 'So long as you don't care who Heather goes out with,' I said gruffly, and he said, 'I couldn't care less, so long as she's got someone responsible for her and she's off my shoulders.' Which ought to have comforted me, only it didn't. He added, with a lop-sided grin, 'I suppose one could say *he* was a responsible person?' and he started to laugh, and the more Richard laughed, the more it hurt to think that Heather could go out in that car with Jeff for the whole evening, when all I wanted was . . .

I shut off that thought in my mind as being despicable. What did it matter what Jeff Watt did with his spare time? He didn't want me, that was quite plain. In fact, it seemed when I thought of what he said at my grandmother's, that all he wanted to see was me safely settled with Richard. And as I'd always wanted Richard, wasn't that a reasonable hope on the part of everyone else, that I would now be happy with him? My grandmother, my friends, especially Frances, all seemed happy as things were now.

And then I remembered something else. 'She saw us, though. It's supposed to be a secret engagement,' I reminded Richard.

'Yes, well, only because Heather herself would have been fed up and made a nuisance of herself, wasn't it?' he protested easily. He found his usual place in the car park and shut off the engine. 'It really is a bit dotty, I suppose, thinking we could keep it a secret in a place like this. Besides, now she's got what she always wanted . . . ' He broke off, and his eyes were troubled, as if he had just thought of a new aspect of it. 'I say, I do wish she hadn't, though,' he said anxiously. 'Why couldn't she have fixed up with Charlie Ross or Driscoll or someone nearer her own age? Someone who'd rush around with her all the time and not care what a pest she was. That's a thought, you know, love! Oh, well, if it really is the lion-tamer she wants, perhaps it'll work out all right.'

I was so astonished to hear him talking like this about Heather, the girl I had thought he was as crazy about as every other man was, that for the moment I missed the significance of his very real anxiety. And yet, besides being anxious, he was still inclined to be amused, a thing which really puzzled me.

When I got to my room, Frances knocked on the door and said, 'I say — did you see Heather just now?' and she looked worried.

I was beginning to feel pretty cross by then, only it was no use taking it out on Frances, and besides, I couldn't very well say that I objected to Heather going around with Jeff. It would have looked so petty, apart from letting Frances know I was keen on him myself. Keen? What a feeble understatement sort of word that is! I felt rather that my heart had been torn out of me and that the place where it had been would never heal, it would go on hurting and hurting for ever.

'What about the lion-tamer?' I asked between my teeth.

'Oh, he's all right. That pretty little

thing who rides the horses bareback — Bianca Something — is with him,' Frances said. 'It seems that her father has had a word with the lion-tamer and reminded him that he's officially engaged to Bianca, so I don't think he'll be seeing Heather alone any more.'

'So she has to find another escort quick, to save face,' I ruminated, rather bitterly.

'I'm sorry,' Frances said, almost as if she knew all about it.

I was sure she couldn't. Anyway, I hoped she didn't. Desperation drove me to say, with a tight throat, 'You might as well know we saw her, so she saw us too, so there isn't any point in keeping a secret of the fact that I'm engaged to Richard.'

Frances seemed stunned. 'You're wha-at?' she managed at last.

'Well, you knew that, didn't you?' I said slowly. 'You said the other day something about I was engaged to someone whose name you weren't supposed to mention?'

She went very red and didn't seem to know what to do. 'Yes, I know, but I wasn't thinking about Richard,' she mumbled. 'Oh, I'd better not say anything else before I put my big foot in it,' which she proceeded to do by adding, 'Anyway, you saw Heather in the car with him and you didn't seem too put out so I suppose I got it all wrong as usual. I think you're more worried about the lion-tamer than him!'

Hospital! It's one big hotbed of gossip! I felt as if I'd been living in a goldfish bowl for ages and only just become aware of it. Had all the patients known, and stared speculatingly at me every day when I washed the helpless and took their temperatures and changed the dressings? Were they, in common with my friends, aware that Heather was now going out with the man I really loved — Jeff — while I was left with Richard, and were they as sorry for me as my friends, for having Jeff snatched from under my nose by Heather?

I felt as if I couldn't face the ward again, but I did. I threw myself into my work. Our ward was very busy but the men didn't stay all that long. A man would be in with apparently every limb in some sort of contraption, from some multiple road smash, and in no time at all, he'd be shedding them one by one, and hobbling about, because we had a thing about getting people on the move and getting the blood circulating again.

Some accident cases took longer than others, of course, but the average was only in for a few weeks, not months like the patients on the medical wards. In some ways I felt this would suit me better. Looking after the helpless was all right so long as they weren't so ill that you had to tiptoe about. The men, no matter what had happened to them, were inclined to quip and joke to keep their ends up. And my junior was a jolly type, too.

In the earlier part of the year I would

have been thrilled with this ward, but now I dreaded Richard's rounds. His quiet, slightly possessive smile bothered me. It was as if he were glad that he had had his mind made up for him about his future — both his job and his wife. The men found out and referred to him as 'my bloke' which didn't help matters, because I kept being quite sure that they knew about Jeff and were being heavily tactful about it, so that it stuck out everywhere.

But luckily I saw very little of Heather.

After a week on that ward, dreading every time Richard looked at me in case he should announce that he had got the marriage licence, I ran into Jeff Watt. Literally ran into him, as we were both hurrying round a corner from opposite directions and the impact was so smart that it sent me spinning and I couldn't get my balance and flopped in a heap on the ground.

It was a cold day and I had had my cloak wrapped round me with no hands left free to save myself. As before he yanked me easily to my feet, and glared at me. He was holding my arms in a grip that hurt, and forgot to let go, and he kept on glaring.

I said the first thing that came into my head. 'You! Why don't you look where you're going, Jeff?' And then somehow I was close against him, held in a grip that hurt, and he was muttering over my head, 'Are you all right? Silly little devil! Rushing about like that!' and it was, for a moment, utter bliss.

It was in the coal yard. A short cut I often used though I wasn't supposed to. Only frosted glass windows frowned down at us, but an evil wind whisked round the corner, flicking his coat. Without actively thinking, I saw it was of thin white material. I broke away from his grasp to consider it further but he said harshly, 'Why the hell are you still here? Why aren't you married and off to Switzerland? Where's Richard?' He gave me a little shake and continued in that angry voice, 'Have you got over that business at the circus when that lion-tamer chap was brought in? How's your arm? Cut it, didn't you? Why the hell don't you stay indoors if you can't keep out of trouble?'

All I could think of was why he should be wearing a white coat and why he should have taken Heather out that day but still be getting angry over me. I said coldly, 'Keep your anxiety for Heather! She likes going out in your Boss's car, so stick with it chum, and leave me alone!'

He looked terribly angry and a bit taken aback, I thought, and somehow not like the Jeff Watt I knew, at all. Jeff always had a rather insolent grin or a wicked twinkle in his eye. This Jeff merely looked sort of frustrated and angry. He said in a low voice, 'Eileen, are you being wilfully stupid or are you just like any other girl, playing me up and pretending you don't understand? I've done all I can for you! I've ordered my stupid nephew to marry you

— that's what you wanted, isn't it? And I even take Heather out, and bore myself to tears, keeping her out of your hair. What more can I do? Why don't you marry Richard and *go*, so I can have some peace again!'

For a minute, I didn't understand, and then suddenly the truth hit me in the face. Why it had never pierced my consciousness before I'll never know. I suppose I was just hanging on to what I wanted to believe. But now there was no escape. I had to see the truth. I repeated dully, 'Your nephew? Did you say your *nephew*?' and I still didn't want to understand.

He looked as if he had said too much; sort of baffled. I don't know what he would have done then or indeed what I would have done. I just stood and stared at him. Someone came out of X-rays and said, 'Oh, there's Sir Russington now!' which just about swept away any more misunderstanding on my part. Footsteps came hurrying, and like a shot he let go of my arms and turned away towards the others.

I watched them. The Casualty Officer, not wearing his usual affable grin but deferential, and Sir Hartley, who took Richard's uncle's arm and spoke earnestly to him as they hurried back. The great man himself, being borne away for a conference or a spot of bother that nobody else could disentangle.

And I, *I*, a little second-year nurse, had had the temerity to be rude to him, to call him 'Jeff', to think he was a dogsbody and to treat him like one — and even fall in love with him!

I tottered back to the Nurses' Home, and all the way, and long after I reached there, I was shivering. I couldn't stop shivering. I sat on my bed and went over that scene. I kept seeing him turn away and walk back with the other two men. I kept thinking of his white coat and how he had stopped looking young and handsome and devil-may-care, the Jeff I knew; he had become older, an important person on hospital ground, and something else — a man who was not happy, a very angry man, a baffled man. And that I didn't understand either.

I thought about it, and could only suppose that he had grown tired of the nonsense of being the dogsbody, in soiled clothes, polishing the brasswork and baiting one of the little second-year nurses, and he had reverted to what he was: the great pathologist, our own important Boffin, not the man who teased me whenever he saw me down by the wharves — the man who was Jeff, my Jeff!

Jeff! The times I had called him Jeff, to his face! But it just wasn't possible. I couldn't accept it. He just couldn't be Richard's uncle. He wasn't old enough to be Richard's uncle . . . was he? It wasn't *possible*.

But it was, wasn't it, though somehow I had got it into my head that this was the man who annoyed me by grinning at me, as he lovingly did cleaning chores aboard that fine craft called *Seamaid II*. Was it possible that the great man would polish his own brasswork? Well, he was said to be eccentric, wasn't he? And it must be him because that fisherman had said that Sir Russington could handle that craft alone in any weather, and was a sight worth watching.

But he couldn't be Sir Russington, my angry shattered thoughts clamoured. Sir Russington was an old man with glasses who crouched in that corner of the Path. Lab. and shouted at unfortunate little nurses. And was never seen by anyone, so that there was a popular story going the rounds that he was ugly or scarred or something. Yet Frances had obviously been hinting that she thought I was keen on him. An old man? Someone had said he was forty . . . who? I concentrated hard on that.

And then I remembered the conversation in Dr Barclay's surgery that day when I had passed out. Shivering from deep cold and shock, I recalled every word of that. Dr Barclay had said that I would never forgive him. For what? Pretending to be the dogsbody of the great man himself? But why, why? Where was the sense of it?

I remembered with acute discomfort the way he had come into my grandmother's cottage the day my arm was hurt, and the way Gran had looked, sort of outraged, I remembered, at the way I was speaking to him, I suppose. She had shook her head at me and asked where my manners were. Yes, he was Sir Russington, and she would know. But why hadn't she mentioned him by name? Perhaps she had been stunned because of my rudeness to him and because I had kept calling him Jeff. Or perhaps, which was more to the point, because he was talking to me in what she would have called a shockingly free manner, and Gran being Gran, would not have said anything, as she didn't understand what on earth was going on.

Jeff. How that name had cropped up, I couldn't remember! And then I seemed to recall that there was a man called Tom Jeffers who worked at the big house on the hill, where Sir Russington lived. I hadn't thought much about him, because I had kept in my mind the picture of a rude, bad-tempered crouching old man, and nothing about him had interested me. But Jeff was what he had been called, and Sir Russington had used that name on the beach that day, and it was I who had said Jeff what? and he had made it into a name. Jeff Watt. Yes, it had been him who had started this deception, and he had deliberately fostered it, playing upon the fact that for some reason I hadn't recognized him. Oh, he must have enjoyed himself, every time he had seen me! And I had fallen in love with him!

I heeled over and buried my shamed face in my hands, and remembered the good days when I had met him on that end of the shore. The day I had got my feet mixed up with the tackle and he had found me crying. The day he had invited me to swim with him but the weather hadn't been fit after that. I remembered the way he had told me to dress as an urchin for the Ball, and his taste and judgment would have been right, I could see that now. Oh, yes, that Ball! He had been dressed as a burglar and conveniently vanished before the unmasking, and he had been so angry with Heather for providing that dingy outfit for me, that she had grandly described as a moth. Oh, and the things I had said to him! My face flamed and I felt I could never go out of my room again and meet anyone.

Then I thought about Heather, riding by him in the big car. Had Heather known who he was? Somehow I thought she did know. She had constantly hinted about my meeting someone down there on the shore all the time, so she must have guessed. Guessed his identity before I did! Of course — I remembered then saying to Heather the day the lion-tamer was hurt, 'I can't see Sir Russington bending any rules on my account, can you?' and she had said coolly, 'Yes, of course'! Oh, yes, Heather had known all right!

Frances came in and said, 'What's up?' because by then I was crying my eyes out. A misery clamped down on me that seemed of never-ending proportions. Whichever way I looked at it, there was no way out, except to quietly leave. Not marry Richard or anyone else. Just leave. How could I marry Richard now, when there was this thing about his uncle?

I savagely mopped my eyes and remembered how he had said at my grandmother's, the day he had carried me down to Richard's father's surgery, that I should have Richard if it was the last thing he did. He must have heard my grandmother talking about my loving Richard since our childhood. And of course, Richard's uncle had been responsible for fixing everything! Oh, what a blind, blind fool I had been, not to see any of it before!

I staggered over to the wash-basin and slopped cold water on my face and said to Frances, between gulps of air, 'I've been the world's biggest ass and I don't think I shall be able to face anyone again!'

She flopped on to the bed as if her legs wouldn't hold her. 'So you know, then?' she said.

'Oh, yes, I know,' I said bitterly, then something in her face struck me as odd, and I said, 'Just a minute, no more talking at cross-purposes. What do you mean you think I know?'

She said, 'About Heather! She's gone.'

'Gone?' I echoed stupidly, and all I could think of was that Sir Russington had taken her away, because I wouldn't go away with Richard. Which was pretty stupid.

Frances said, 'Yes, the lion-tamer went today and people are saying she followed him, but personally I think that's the end. I mean, she might be silly over him because of his muscles and his being so masculine — you know what she's like. And she might get a kick out of lifting him from his girl-friend. But she wouldn't want to stay with him. Not her! She's on the look-out for a rich beau. She's said so often enough.' And then poor Frances put her hands to her hot face, because no doubt she was thinking, as I was, that we had both seen Heather sitting by Richard's uncle in his big car, and that would be triumph for Heather if she could pull off something like that.

Well, he was rich. Handsome, too, and very masculine. But would the restless Heather settle for someone tied to his work as Sir Russington was? And that much older than her, too?

'He's nearly forty,' I said flatly, and Frances didn't even bother to ask me who I was talking about. She knew.

'When are you and Richard going to get married?' she asked bluntly, and I said, 'I don't know. After this, I don't think I shall marry anyone,' which reminded her that she still didn't know what had upset me.

And I couldn't tell her. I kept seeing in my mind, pictures of me being an absolute ass, like that day when Richard pointed out his uncle crossing the gates in front of the hospital and all I could see was Jeff, and I didn't connect the two. And I thought of the nice times, like Jeff making me pay for his tea at the stall down by the harbour because I had argued about him paying for me. And the time he had danced with me and I was so breathless with the agonizing excitement his nearness always stirred in me that I could hardly speak. I turned to the window, keeping my back to Frances and I said shortly, 'I've had the father and mother of all rows with Sir Russington, if you want to know. I shall have to leave, of course.'

She didn't say anything. She just sat there, waiting to hear more, I suppose. After all, she was my friend. But I just wanted her to go. I just wanted to be alone and to go back over everything to see if I could find something that would disclose to me how I could have been such a fool as to think he was the chauffeur, and then I suddenly remembered how he had talked to me that first time, as if he really had been another person, and I remembered distinctly that he had definitely kidded me along that his boss was someone quite different. Oh, yes, he had intended that deception! And I had fallen for it.

I turned sharply and muttered, 'I've got to pack. I'm leaving now, before I can change my mind.'

Frances sat and watched me, with a sort of hopeless look on her face. 'You don't want to go haring after Heather,' she said at last, with wonderment in her voice.

I said bitterly, 'I do not! In fact, I don't care if I never hear of Heather again in my whole life!'

Absently she got up and started taking things out of the drawers I hadn't started on yet. She was a neat and tidy packer. She also took out the things I had slung into my two cases and started folding them, putting soft smalls into my shoes and rolling them in newspaper, to keep them from my clean underwear and nighties. I gave it up, my hands were shaking too much anyway.

Frances said, 'I suppose you don't want to unload, about what the row was over? I mean, you were saying you didn't know what Sir Russington looked like, not so long ago. When did you find out?'

I choked on the word 'today'. I couldn't bear to admit it. I just shook my head and begged her to leave me alone.

'I'll get you some tea,' she said, and started off for the tiny kitchen at the end of our corridor.

I don't know how long elapsed before she came back again. That was a day of things being highlighted, so that they stood out for no reason. Little things, like the sight of Heather in the distance this morning, only I hadn't remembered it before. She had looked dejected, I now remembered. Over the lion-tamer? What had she expected? That the father of the girl wouldn't make a push to ensure that his daughter married the man she was engaged to? That they would take in a stranger like Heather, into their close little world? Heather certainly had wanted show business, but the world of the circus and the animal tamers was so sharply distinctive. She must have known she wouldn't fit in, and she must have known they wouldn't have her just because she had the whim to take that man from his girl. I kept remembering her laughing that day when I had thought she was crying, and she had told me it made her feel better to know she could get a man on her side in — what had she said? Oh, yes, thirty seconds flat. I found I was disliking her more than ever.

I remembered, too, that Richard hadn't looked very happy when I had seen him crossing the yard below the ward window. That may or may not have been because his work was on his mind. I didn't know. But I hadn't even seen him to speak to, and somehow the business of our marriage had not been taken up since that day we had looked at the engagement rings. Wasn't he so enthusiastic any more?

Quite suddenly I had a revulsion for going through with it. I would have to stop it. Never mind that I had been made a fool of, over the identity of his uncle. I just couldn't marry Richard. I wanted Gran. I had to get home.

And all the while, at the back of my mind, was the question: why had Heather run off? It wasn't like her. She could brazen anything out. There were any amount of young men to take away from their girls, all the fun imaginable left for her, here in the world of hospital. There was, too, the matter of that brooch, the Golden Butterfly? She had either discovered who had given it to her, or perhaps Sir Russington had said something sharp to her. All of a sudden I felt that that was what had happened. I remembered at this late stage, too, how he had told me he had taken her on to let me and Richard get away, and that it was a burden he need not have bothered with. Something like that.

I was ready. I decided not to stop and change out of my uniform in case Frances came back and tried to dissuade me from going. My cases were strapped and ready, and all I had to do now was to find someone to take me to the station. I made to lift the two cases but I couldn't raise them. I tried again. It was my injured arm that wouldn't take the weight of the biggest case. A slow frightening pain gripped it and stayed. I panicked. I had sat down again when Frances returned with the tea. I said, my voice choky, 'I can't lift them. They're too heavy. My arm, my stupid arm!' and she put the tea down and sat looking at me, then she put her arms round me and I think we were both crying a bit.

Then she pushed me off. 'Oh, this is

soppy! We must pull ourselves together. What am I thinking of? You can't leave, not without going to Matron first. You owe that courtesy to her. If you're afraid of Sir Russington barging in, don't be. He went out. I saw his car not long ago. Why don't you go down and have a heart-to-heart with Matron, and I'll see if Charlie Ross is around? I think he is. I'll ask him to drive you.'

She turned rather pink as she said it. I repeated, 'Charlie Ross? He's Heather's property!' but Frances said, tautly, 'Not any more. He's fed up with her giving him the run-around. He's . . . he's sort of going to be my property. He's rather nice, actually.'

This was yet another shock, but my own fault. She was supposed to be my friend but I'd been so taken up with Richard and his uncle and Heather lately, that I hadn't had time to see what Frances was making of her life. I said, 'Well, better he has you than her. He deserves you.' I don't think I'd got it the right way round but she took it as a compliment and looked rather pleased, and she went off to find him. But she didn't get far.

She joined the hurrying feet, and the ambulance siren and the unmistakable sounds of a three-star emergency.

Everyone goes, when there are those noises. A three-star accident calls everyone out, on duty or off. I forgot that I was on my way to leaving the hospital. I forgot that my arm wasn't working as it should have. I went, too. Joining the others who came running, and glad I hadn't stopped to change out of my uniform.

It has always puzzled me how word gets around, what has happened. A policeman was down there in Casualty, and Casualty Sister looked perturbed, not a usual thing with that bland person. They both looked over at me. Well, in my direction, but I felt that it was at me they were looking, and I immediately felt that it was Jeff who was the centre of the emergency. Well, Frances had seen him driving out of the hospital gates, hadn't she? I felt a pain in the pit of my stomach and I couldn't move.

But it wasn't him. I saw him come striding in a little later. I saw Frances, too, and she looked terrible, just as if someone in the accident belonged to her, and that thoroughly unnerved me, for Frances, like Sister Casualty, didn't get upset easily.

I don't know much of what happened then, or just how I heard it, but Heather's name was being bandied about. I gathered from here and there, as I tried to help, that she had cadged a lift from a passing motorist who had been involved in a four-car pile-up on our highly controversial motorway. But it still didn't answer why Frances should have looked upset.

Richard came by soon after that, and it was he who told me. One of the cars in the pile-up had been driven by Charlie Ross.

9

Frances's Charlie, and our Golden Butterfly! I felt very sick. Richard was at my side. He was as calm as ever, very much in charge of the situation, I noticed. 'Go upstairs, Eileen. I don't want you down here,' he said firmly.

But he was only Richard who I had known all my life so I fallen helplessly in love with him because I had only gone I said indignantly, and I didn't really realize then how ill I looked or that my injured arm was hanging in an odd way. Richard was looking at it. 'Go back,' he said again.

'I'm all right!' I protested. 'I just picked up something heavy and it jerked my bad arm, but it'll be all right. Don't fuss me, Richard! Besides, Frances is here. If she can be of use, so can I.'

'Take her with you,' he surprised me

by saying. 'I don't want her to see Ross. Not yet, anyway. Take her away, there's a good girl.'

That was different, so I nodded, and went over to where I had seen her vanish. Richard went off in another direction, confident that I would do as he had told me to.

Frances was in a cubicle where a girl was lying. It was nobody we knew. Just another of the people involved. Frances was cleaning up the girl's face.

It's funny, I thought, as I took a bowl and started doing the same thing to the girl's leg. By the time one is second year, certain things have become ingrained. A cook will automatically start to beat fat and sugar together; a Second Year faced by a casualty will automatically get a bowl and things and start cleaning up.

The Casualty Officer came in behind us, looking quickly at me, and said affably, 'Ah, there you are! Been looking for you everywhere. Clear out, Eileen! Sir Russington says so. *Stat*.' And

Frances looked at me and nodded, so I went. She looked better by then and I knew it was no use arguing. Also my bad arm was now beginning to throb. Why? It was supposed to be healed.

Everybody seemed to have heard about this accident, I saw, on my way back through the hospital to the Nurses' Home. People stopped me, one after another, and asked about Heather. That astonished me. They didn't ask about Charlie Ross, who was such a nice chap, always cheerful and helpful. No, just about Heather. The general idea was that she had been ticked off by someone and hadn't liked it and had decided to run off somewhere and start afresh. I couldn't believe it.

Someone said there was a telephone call for me. I took it. It was Richard's father. 'Eileen, is that you? Look, I can't get hold of Richard. They tell me there's a flap on.'

'Yes, there is. It's Heather,' I said. 'I don't know how she is, only that she was in a motorway crash.'

Then he said, in a funny voice, 'Eileen, you don't sound too good. Richard . . . he wasn't with her, was he?'

I was so surprised. 'No, he's helping in Casualty. Why should he have been with her? He's engaged to me, remember?'

'Yes. Yes, I know that,' he said, and he sounded so agitated that I started to think that something else was wrong.

I said, 'It's Gran, isn't it? Is she ill? Dr Barclay, is it Gran? You must tell me!' and I could hear my voice rising.

'No, she's all right,' he said, 'but you're not, are you? Upset about your friend Heather, are you?'

My *friend*! The question floored me. I didn't know how to answer that one.

I leaned my hot forehead against the wall where the telephone was suspended. The long, long corridor stretched to eternity at each end. Murmured sounds, cosy sounds, came from the wards. Casualty seemed a long way away. And I felt very much alone and uncertain and unhappy at that moment, and angry because of this queer weakness that was creeping over me.

I said at last, 'Of course there's nothing wrong with me!' more to reassure myself, and I added, 'And no, I am not upset about her in particular. It's something else, and to be frank, if this pile-up hadn't happened, I was on my way out, home to Gran. And it's your fault, too!' I burst out suddenly.

He paused, surprised, I suppose. Then he said very gently, 'What is it, Eileen? Not fallen out with Richard, have you?'

'Richard! Richard! That's all anyone says! All my life I've thought of nothing but Richard! But he's not like I thought he was — he's just letting himself be pushed around because his uncle — ' And then all the soreness inside me, the great lump of ice that ought to have been my heart, all seemed to burst out into one great question to poor puzzled Dr Barclay. 'Why, *why* didn't you tell me? About his uncle! I never knew! I can't stay here now, not after the things I've said to that man! Why didn't someone tell me?'

'Eileen, I think I'm coming over to see about this,' he said at last. 'You're not well, I can tell that. Just stay where you are and I'll fetch you. A week or two at your Gran's will do you all the good in the world, under my eye, too. I ought never to have let you go back so soon after that last lot.'

It seemed to me then, that it was no use going back to Gran's either, because the Barclay family were there, on the doorstep. I would run into them, particularly into *him*.

I said, 'No, don't do that. Nobody will want to know about me while this flap's on. Later, when it's sorted out, I'll come back for the week-end and see you,' and I hung up, and only when the receiver was back on its hook did I realize that he hadn't said why he had wanted Richard or why he had thought Richard was in the accident with Heather.

The way I was feeling scared me a little. I didn't want to go to back to my room. I felt vaguely that I would be better if I were in the swim of things, so I returned to Casualty. There were still a lot of people milling about, and someone who hadn't known of my being ordered out of the place, gave me a comparatively light but none the less useful job, that of seeing to the walking patients involved. They were getting in the way, trying to buttonhole busy people to ask questions. There was, for instance, a driver of one of the cars. He had got off lightly, but he was very upset. A man in his middle thirties, his rather ornately cut but expensive suit blood-spattered, he had only bruises and cuts himself and he had been treated and told to sit still.

He couldn't. He wanted to talk, and I didn't want him to get hold of the ever-eager junior reporter who was usually to be found hanging about the policeman when one of these pile-ups occurred. The motorway was too near our town. The local paper was always trying to make something of that fact, and this would be yet another axe to grind.

The patient said his name was Philip Holford, and waited, as if he expected me to have heard of it before. It did sound familiar, but I couldn't place it then, so he said, 'It was nothing to do with the motorway. It's a good road. No, it was all my fault.'

'I wouldn't say that, if I were you,' I warned him. 'Not till you feel better.' But I let him talk, just the same. He wanted to.

He sipped the hot sweet tea I'd got him and he told me a girl with glorious curly dark hair had flagged him down for a lift.

Heather. There was no doubt about that, and later he mentioned her name. He'd stopped and picked her up and heard her life story in a matter of minutes. Like every other man, he was goo-ey about her.

'One of our student nurses. I think she was running away,' I said. 'What did she tell you?'

'Oh, no, she wasn't running away,' he said at once. 'She told me where she was going. She wanted to get into Nosterbridge. Apparently the shops keep open later there, and she had this brooch thing she wanted valued.'

My heart contracted. The Golden Butterfly. So it had spelt disaster for her, too. I suppose I must have said it aloud. He nodded. 'She wanted to raise a lot of money on it for some chap with an act — lions, I think she said — I say,' he broke off with great anxiety. 'It wasn't — well, I mean to say, it did belong to her, didn't it? I only glanced at it but it looked valuable to me!'

'Oh, yes, it belonged to her all right. A secret admirer gave it to her. Everyone tells her she should keep it in the safe in the Hospital Secretary's room,' I said, hardly noticing what I was saying, I was so shocked with what had been in Heather's mind at the time.

'Oh, goodness, what happened to it?' I thought to ask him.

'She was hanging on to it,' he said, 'I don't think she let go. She was showing it to me when all this happened. He put his face in his hands. 'I suppose I just took my eyes off the road for a second to look at it. I don't know, though.' He looked up at me, and I kept thinking how familiar his face was, and how good-looking he was. I didn't think Heather had really meant all that about the new act for the lion-tamer. She probably, I told myself basely, just picked out this young man to flag down, and chose the lion-tamer for the story to interest him. And then, as always, I felt mean.

'Don't worry about it now,' I advised him.

'But I can't see how it could have happened. This lorry seemed to come right across the bonnet of my car. I couldn't do a thing to avoid it. I think it must have skidded from the other lane, and over the crash barrier. I can't be quite sure.' He rubbed his eyes. 'Oh, what a mess! I've never had anything happen before this. I'm a careful driver. You must know that! Everyone must!'

I didn't see why, so I asked him gently, 'What's your job?'

He told me. It was ironical. No wonder his name was familiar, even to me, a desultory cinema-goer. He was a well-known actor-manager. And just the sort of person Heather would want to know!

He kept on about Heather, of course; her fascination, the friendly way she had talked to him, the fascinating way she had looked as she had thumbed a lift. He never picked up girls, he said, but he felt he couldn't resist this one. Oh, well, that was Heather!

I let him talk, and finally I was called away to help in a cubicle, and our cub reporter was ploughing his way through to Philip Holford. He had recognized him. He wouldn't get much out of Philip, though. He was too upset, thinking about the girl he had picked up and wondering whether she would survive.

Myself, I had not dared to think about that. And it did seem a wry trick of Fate that because word had got around that my arm wasn't fit for lifting, I was given the job of sitting by Heather when she came down from theatre. The last job I wanted.

She had the top of her head bandaged, and her eyes. Nothing else appeared to have been touched. But she had lost all that dark curly hair, and she looked unfamiliar.

'Is she going to be blind?' I heard myself ask, and someone said, 'Oh, we hope not! It's early days. Just you sit there and don't move that arm — it will be all right if you rest it.'

I sat looking stupidly at her, and thinking, what would I say if she came round and wanted to know what had happened? Heather didn't have disasters happen to her. Heather, of all people, to be like this!

People kept remembering her as she

had been; full of life, always up to something that made everyone else furious. Always with a new boy-friend in tow. Nobody blamed her for anything, now. The passing of people who just looked in to peep at her, was staggering. Not just nurses and up-patients, but housemen and students, the Big Shots, even Richard's uncle.

I knew it was him before he came in. I recognized his walk and my heart started to pep up its beat and I felt sick in the pit of my stomach. I prayed he wouldn't come in. I heard his voice, saying a thing or two in a low murmur to Sister, outside the door. I heard my name mentioned. 'Jeff, Jeff,' my nerves screeched, 'don't come in! I can't bear it! *Go away!*'

But of course he would come in. He was Heather's latest man on a string, wasn't he?

He came in and stood behind me as I sat by the bed, and he put his hands on my shoulders, hard, and the grip of his fingers sent sparks all through me, and I closed my eyes and felt faint. I whispered, 'Go away! Don't touch me!' but he whispered back, 'Must see you. Want to talk to you,' and then he went. It had been me he'd wanted to see, not Heather, apparently.

I wilted in my chair. I was torn in two. I wanted to see him, yet I didn't. I had tried, hadn't I, to get away, only this had happened! Why couldn't I have just gone, so I wouldn't have known about this?

Sitting there, I knew I would give up nursing. I think Gran had always known I would. I suppose I had only become a nurse because Richard had been a doctor. I had had to share his world, without realizing he didn't need me. Come to think of it, how on earth had I been so blind as to not notice that Richard didn't really need anyone? He was a happy doctor. Nothing shattered him, I remembered. His world of medicine was not a sorry place that was always on the losing side. He was always filled with the hope that just round the corner (thanks to his formidable uncle and others like him) were wonderful things to be discovered, to cure everything. And meantime he did his best, with the tools to hand. No feeling sick or inadequate for Richard. And what sort of a wife would I have made him?

I tried to tell a lot of this to Matron later, when I was freed from Heather's bedside. I didn't attempt to see Sir Russington. Matron had sent for me, so I went to her at once. Apparently she was incensed that someone had been so stupid as to give me the job of specialling Heather, as she thought, poor woman, that I was so close to Heather that it must have been terribly upsetting for me.

'No, Matron,' I said, standing in front of her desk in the approved fashion, arms folded behind me (at least, the good one). Other hospitals might have innovations about the Matron kindly asking the nurse to sit, but not in ours. Matron was the Big Shot on the nursing side, and we stood to denote respect. 'No, Matron, I am not close enough to Heather to be upset.'

'But it was you who wanted so badly to have her in the hospital — a wish which moved not only Dr Richard Barclay but his uncle, Sir Russington, to speak for the girl, nurse!'

'I believe so, Matron, but I thought . . . well, you may think this doesn't sound very responsible, but looking back, I'm afraid her personality was such . . . well, Richard and I (I mean, Dr Barclay and I) we both thought the other wanted her as a nurse, and we both . . . well, I think we were brainwashed by her. She does that to everyone. She gets what she wants, all the time.'

But not this time, my heart beat out unhappily. Things had gone very wrong for Heather, for once.

Matron said as much.

'Just the same. I didn't mind sitting by her, Matron,' I protested, 'but what upset me more than that, was about my best friend, Nurse Trepple. She's friends with Dr Ross, and he was injured in that accident, too, and that upset me more than what happened to Nurse Maple.'

'Yes,' Matron agreed, and looked at her hands; they were threatening to break her biro in two, which wasn't like Matron. Something cried out inside me. Surely poor Charlie Ross was in a bad way for Matron to look like that! And it was all through Heather and her cadging a lift to get at the value of that damned brooch.

Matron said, 'Dr Ross, as with other unfortunate people, was caught up in this through nobody's fault. As to you and your future, I hope you are not going to propose something I shan't be able to agree with, nurse. You have the makings of a good nurse in you, and we all have a jolt like this at some time or other.'

If she hadn't stopped there, I would have broken in. I couldn't hold out any longer.

'I want to leave, Matron. I was on the point of leaving when this happened. I don't know why Dr Ross was out in his car. My friend Nurse Trepple had gone to look for him to give me a lift with my luggage. Oh, yes, I know I should have come to you first, but I was afraid I wouldn't be allowed to leave — I mean, Sir Russington — '

I don't know how I managed to get that man's name out, but I did, and she nodded. 'I agree with you, Nurse, Sir Russington would have had something to say about it. And that was another thing I had to speak to you about. But I'm afraid it will have to wait now,' and she got up, her eyes turning to the door behind me, as if someone else was there.

I glanced back. There was nobody there now. She had gone out with whoever had opened that door.

I leaned my hands on the back of the chair in front of me, and took a little rest. I didn't feel too good. I wondered what was the matter with me. I knew, I think, standing there, that I should never be fit enough to finish my training. I had been so strong and gay and carefree before Heather came. That bout of illness at Gran's had sapped not only the strength out of me, but the heart out of me, too. Battling with Heather was like the man in the fable, who kept cutting off the giant's limbs but more grew again to hold swords to fight the poor man with. He never won. And I would never win.

I felt sick. I didn't want to wait to hear any more of Matron's homilies or to see Sir Russington. I was sure that he would be here at any minute and I felt too weak to fight him again.

Matron's room was a pleasant one on the ground floor, with french windows behind her desk, opening on to a rose garden. I went out that way, without thought. I just had to get out.

The touch of the wind was like icy fingers that ripped at me. I shot through the garden, and out into the car park, but by the time I reached the

Nurses' Home my teeth were chattering. I was an idiot, I knew, and I'd be in shocking trouble all round, but there was just so much I could take, and no more.

I knew I'd never be able to get out of my uniform, the way my arm was feeling, nor would I be able to pick up and carry any luggage, so I grabbed up my top coat and shrugged it round me, and my handbag, and went down to find a taxi. There should be one somewhere.

There was better than that. There was my friend the laundry-van driver, and he was full of the news that his wife was expecting a baby, a baby he wanted born in our hospital. He had no interest in the crash, which everyone was talking about. He didn't even notice how awful I looked, nor did he find it odd that I should require a lift to the station. I let him talk. When he dropped me, I somehow got into the booking hall, bought a ticket and caught a train within minutes, back to Gran's. My refuge. My home.

Isn't it funny, how one turns to home the minute one is in trouble or feeling ill? I knew it wasn't sensible in my case. With Richard and his father and his formidable uncle almost on the door-step, what refuge did I expect at Gran's? But that was where I wanted to go. I don't remember much about the journey or my arrival. I only remember vaguely seeing Gran at the door, looking upset. The light had faded out of that bitter cold day, and then I was in my own bed at Gran's, and Gran's voice scolding lovingly, and I was very, very warm. Too warm, really, and oddly chill inside me.

Gran's panacea for all ills is to keep the patient warm. Warm blankets, hot-water bottles, hot things to drink. But that was wrong in this instance. I heard Richard's father telling her I had a very high temperature and had to be sponged down at regular intervals.

Dr Barclay also seemed to know what had been happening at the hospital, so that was all right, I remembered thinking drowsily. I wouldn't have to go through the whole beastly story again. I could sink down into the darkness and not bother about any of them. Not bother if Heather was going to be able to see . . .

The thought jerked me up from the cosy darkness. What a thing to think! Of course I must find out how Heather was! Another thought jerked at me. I must find out whether my friend Frances Trepple's Dr Ross was going to survive or be a cripple, through Heather's latest effort to do what she wanted to! What made me think I needn't bother? Not bother about the fact that Richard's uncle had been taking Heather out? Not bother about what had happened to that highly expensive brooch, the Golden Butterfly, and more important, who had given it to her? Ill as I was, in that moment, I thought I knew who had given it to her. Sir Russington himself. I don't know why I came to that conclusion: perhaps because it was the one thing I didn't want to believe.

Never mind, I consoled myself confusedly. I was in my bed at Gran's and Richard's father was attending me. So it would be all right. I'd bother about all those things later, much later.

But very soon I was no longer in my bed at Gran's. Most uncomfortably I was made fully aware of this. I was lying on a hard narrow bed that bumped and lurched, with a nurse sitting by me, and someone who's eyes were remarkably like Jeff's, sat by me, too, only I couldn't be sure, because he and the nurse were all covered in white — even caps and masks. It was a horrible, horrible nightmare that ended with a bang, and a great cold wind rushed in on me and bright lights, and more people, masked.

It was much later that I realized this was the transition from ambulance to hospital, and then only because I recognized it as our hospital. I was then warm, in a bed that didn't bump or lurch, and there were plain glass windows high in the partition that separated my small room from the passage, and I recognized the special shaped crack in the wall as the one outside the Medical Wing, a special part of the Medical Wing in which I had never worked.

The old terror filled me, that used to fill us when we had been young ones in the Training School, and we didn't know any better and used to scare ourselves with the thought of what it would be like to be actually lying in a hospital bed, really being the patient, and young untrained nurses advancing towards us with villainous-looking instruments. We used to frighten each other in those days, and then take it in turns to be the guinea pig; it was only for blanket baths and simple things like that, but I could still feel the thrill of fear when I was flat on my back playing at being the patient and Frances was bending over me pretending to be an S.R.N.

And now I was really flat on my back, in one of those beds. I stared at that odd-shaped crack and knew where it was, and because I knew that it was the Medical Wing Annexe, a new fear filled me, because when a nurse is ill, she goes to the Sick Bay in the Nurses' Home.

★   ★   ★

This was Sir Russington's experimental unit. It was some days before I realized that. It was connected to the main hospital block by a high bridge; virtually isolated. And it wasn't difficult to be aware of it, either, because barrier nursing was in progress. Everyone who came in wore a white gown, cap and mask. I lay sweating, wondering what disease I'd got, to need such a thing, and because I was worrying about the matter of contagion, I lost sight of the fact that little by little my limbs were refusing to obey me.

The realization that I was helpless

lying there, came so gradually, all mixed up with a nightmare of Jeff by my bed, his arms round me, saying brokenly, 'Eileen, Eileen, what have you done?' and to my confused mind he seemed to be blaming me for Heather losing her sight. That crazy idea stuck and grew and wouldn't shift.

I had numberless injections; there were countless hours when I remembered nothing. I learned how to recognize the people I knew, above those masks and behind those white gowns, by watching the eyes. How often do we really look at a person's eyes, enough to recognize that person when the colour of the hair, the style of dress, everything distinctive, has become anonymous beneath the covering of white? The only eyes I really had any interest in were Jeff's and he came many times. Several times a day, and every day.

I croaked at him one day, 'Why do you bother with me? You were so angry with me! Why don't you go to Heather?'

But as always weak tears swamped my eyes and face and I didn't see the reaction in his, nor hear what he said.

One day I recognized Richard's eyes. He said softly, 'Hello, love, what on earth has been happening to you?' But in my shattered state I thought he'd come to talk about marriage, and I heard myself say in a fevered voice, 'Don't want to marry you, Richard. Want *him*. Where *is* he?'

'Who, love?' Richard asked gently.

'You won't fetch him for me, I know you won't. You want me to marry you,' I sobbed.

'No, love, no, of course I don't,' he assured me. 'I gave up the idea when you told me you loved someone else.'

'You mean that?' I wept.

'Of course, my love. Don't worry.'

'What will you do?'

Richard said firmly, 'I'll be fine. I've got my work. Never wanted to be married yet, anyway. I'll be just fine. Just you tell me who this chap is you want, and I'll fetch him for you.'

But I couldn't of course. It was hopeless.

I resolved to ask Richard next day all the things I wanted to know. There was so much I wanted to know: things like what did Gran think about the things that were happening to me? Was she worried or hadn't they told her? What had happened to Charlie Ross and Frances? And what about Heather and the other people in that crash. But Richard didn't come when I was awake and on the look-out for him, and nobody else would answer my questions.

They did read bits of Gran's letters to me, sometimes, but I always got the feeling that they were selected bits. Things like 'Be a good girl and tell them everything they want to know, so that you can get better quickly,' meant nothing to me. I didn't know what Gran was talking about.

As the days wore on, I got steadily and quietly worse, and I thought of Jeff as a shadow which had gone into the past, and Sir Russington was the enemy, the man who relentlessly asked me stupid questions I felt too ill to be bothered with. When you are feeling as if a little of your strength is ebbing away day by day, you just can't tell someone where you went on your time off two, three weeks ago.

'I didn't do anything wrong,' I made the effort to say. 'I came in on time. I didn't break bounds. I kept with my friends.' But that wasn't what Sir Russington wanted to hear.

He wore, as well as the mask and gown, thick-rimmed glasses, which made him look severe, and it wasn't difficult to think of him as Richard's famous uncle, and not my friend Jeff. And always, after I had slipped away from the grasp of that waspish tongue of his, and his never-ending questions, he got up and looked angrier than ever, or frustrated, or something. I got the feeling he thought I was keeping something secret.

One day near Christmas, Frances

came. I was so thrilled, I tried to lift my arm to wave to her as she stood hesitating at the door, but my arm lay like a lump of lead beside me. I was scared, but it was no use asking her what was the matter with me. Nobody stayed long enough for questions from me. I managed, 'How are you?' and she said she was fine.

I wanted so badly to ask how Dr Ross was, but I couldn't make the words come. And it was rather off-putting, because she began to ask the same questions of me that Sir Russington did. 'Where have you been, Eileen? You must try and remember!'

'In bed, of course!' I said, because it was a silly question.

One day she caught me sleeping. I awoke to find her bending over me. I knew her eyes. They had always been brimful of laughter once. Because I had just woken up, I forgot to be careful, and asked outright, 'How's your Charlie Ross?'

She looked absurdly pleased. 'Why,

you remember!' she said. 'He isn't at all bad. Walks with a stick, but he'll get better, they say. And it doesn't really matter for a doctor, does it?' she laughed. 'I mean, it won't stop him driving about, and he's going to get really well soon.' And she said, because I was awake, I suppose, 'Listen! What's that?'

I listened obediently. 'Carols? Christmas carols?' and she nodded. Was it possible, I wondered, that Christmas was on us while I was like this?

I was going to ask some more things, but she ruined it by slipping in that same old question again. 'Think, Eileen. It is important to know where you've *been*.' So I said indignantly, 'Nowhere. Richard and I are finished. Not going to be married: I told him so. How can I marry anyone? I can't move. Why can't I move?'

She looked all fussed and turned away. I was going to lose her, just because I'd asked a question she didn't want to answer. And there were so many more. I tried to shout, but only managed to croak: 'Where's Heather? Can she see?'

I didn't think Frances would stop to answer, but she did. She skidded to a halt and came back. 'Didn't you know she'd had another operation on her eyes? She's all right now. Didn't they tell you?'

'All right now?' I repeated. 'Up?' and she nodded. 'Come to see me?' I suggested, though why I wanted Heather, I didn't quite know, except that there was a half-formed idea that Heather would answer my questions, without the slightest compunction. But that didn't come off. Frances shook her head to that one.

'No, Sir Russington wouldn't allow that, would he,' I croaked and she looked embarrassed. 'Mustn't let the bride come near me, must we?' I thrust at her, hoping that would fetch something, but she merely looked surprised above her mask, and went out quickly.

Well, so now I knew. Heather hadn't lost her sight, she was up and about, and she had taken my dear Jeff from right under my nose and was going to marry him. No wonder he looked cross with me all of the time. He didn't even like me any more.

I lay there thinking of the man I had once known as Jeff, and now in my mind I had completely separated him from Sir Russington. I no longer let myself think they were both the same person. Sir Russington was the important pathologist, who for some reason best known to himself, kept coming to sit by me, examining my useless limbs and asking me questions about where I'd been. Jeff was the man who had irritated me, been friends with me, mopped up my tears when I had wanted Richard, and given me little memories of laughter and camaraderie, walking in the wind, hair wet from the sea, arguments over who should pay for a cup of tea — tea which was better than ever I remembered. Jeff was the one who had carried me, injured from Gran's cottage to Dr Barclay's — Jeff was the strong man, the only one I had ever met. Jeff dancing with me as the burglar in the comic striped jersey, eyes glinting wickedly behind his black mask. Jeff was the one who wanted me to go to that dance as an urchin. Jeff was the man I loved and wanted so badly . . .

It was while I was lying there thinking over these things one day, that I heard voices. There was a screen across the door, and the door had opened a little. One of the speakers had been about to come in. I heard one of them say, 'Nevertheless, until I can find out everywhere she's been, I cannot be certain . . . ' and the other voice said, 'Perhaps we haven't made her understand that she must recall every small insignificant place. I suppose a street market, or something like that, might answer the purpose, but no, she wouldn't have been in such a place long enough,' and the other voice said curtly,

'It only needs half an hour to pick up this bug.'

I had picked up a bug, I told myself. One of Sir Russington's bugs? But his bugs, as every little nurse knew, were to do with paralysis. Fear ripped through me. So that was it!

I was paralysed.

I took it like a blow in the face. I don't think I'd realized why my arms wouldn't come up to wave to Frances any more. Or why people insisted on doing absolutely everything for me. I shut my eyes so I wouldn't have to look at him as he sat down by my side, but his magnetism pushed through the white gown and the mask and he was again my dear Jeff. I needed him, I was so frightened.

'*Jeff!*' I heard myself croak. 'Jeff! Do something! Help me!'

He took my hands in his. I couldn't feel his touch any more and that scared me more than anything else.

'Dear love,' he whispered, 'I can't help you if you won't help me! I've tried everything I know, but I'm working in the dark. I don't know where you picked it up and without that knowledge . . . Think, *think*! Where have you been lately?'

At last I understood those odd questions that had been fired at me for so long.

He added, perhaps because it had suddenly occurred to him, 'Not just where you've been by yourself, but with other people. Your friend Nurse Trepple, for instance? Or Heather?'

I tried, but now a new fear had crept in. I knew, from what I had sometimes heard about the Path. Lab. people, that paralysis crept and crept, and that finally people couldn't even talk if the throat muscles seized up. I dare not let myself think any further, but it almost stopped me thinking at all, just with fright.

He gripped my hands tight. I could see the knuckles of his hands going white, so I knew that. Then he shook his head slightly and let them go. He *knew* I could feel nothing.

Sister had gone out again. He suddenly dropped his face his hands. Oh, how I wanted to touch his crisp dark hair, to see it with drops of salt water in again, as he had been that day on the beach! If only I could have gone in the sea, swum with him that day, to have yet another thing to remember. If only he had kissed me, just once. He called me 'dear love' just now and that had seemed right and proper, like the night at the dance when we had hidden behind the chairs and talked in fierce whispers. It was as if all the bright good things of life were slipping away before my eyes. And I didn't want it to be so, I passionately didn't want it.

I made a determined effort. I remembered silly little trips with Frances and the others, to out of the way shops and dingy museums, flea-pit cinemas in small towns nearby, bus trips, anything, to convince myself I was pulling my weight in remembering. But I could see that nothing I said helped.

I said, 'This is getting as bad as Heather, when she told that woman the awful things that dirt and germs and elderly pet animals and dead birds can do to people. She scared her,' and then I knew I had said something. His head shot up.

'What woman?' he asked, and I strove to think of her name but I couldn't. I had almost forgotten the incident, and I was so tired.

But I had to try. 'I'd gone to an old patient's house to see if the animals were all right. One cage had dead birds in it and I cleaned it out, and that was where Heather found the poster of the lion-tamer and then we went to the circus . . . '

'This old patient, what was her name? Where was the house?' he insisted, but I couldn't remember.

'Rope Lane? Ship Street? Oh, I don't know. Somewhere down near the water. Heather would know — she kept saying there were rats and things. She didn't like it.'

'Heather!' he exclaimed. 'Of course! Why didn't I think of asking *her*?'

He got up and went, his stride taking him to the door in no time at all. The light went out of my day, as always, when he went.

He didn't come back until night-time, with a kidney bowl and syringe. Another of those hated injections! But this time he seemed to hesitate. There was a young man behind him, also gowned. And Sister. Someone was at the door. Sister went behind the screen to it. I heard the young man say, 'Go on, Uncle, for heaven's sake! This is Eileen, our Eileen! What are you waiting for?' *Richard!*

'She's also my guinea pig,' I thought I heard him say. 'The first to be tried.'

'Well, ask her if she wants to be!' Richard said bracingly, and he looked at me. 'Eileen, can you hear me, love? It's me, old Richard — it's the first time we've used this. The very first! You do want it, don't you? Tell him to have faith in himself!'

I heard myself say, on a thread of sound, 'Please, Jeff. I trust you! *Please!*'

Richard said, in a mystified voice, 'What's she calling you Jeff for, sir? Is she delirious?' but I didn't hear any more.

Sometimes during the night hours after that I woke up to find him at my bedside, and I would try to say 'Jeff' but he didn't seem to hear me. Sometimes he was sitting, staring at me. Once he was on his knees by the bedside, but on hearing soft footsteps approaching, he was up in no time, and prowling around the room when Sister came in. But I had seen him close to me, on his knees, and the thought warmed me.

And once I heard him whisper, 'Eileen, dear love, you must live — for me!'

*   *   *

That was just eight months ago. Since then my dear Jeff has become famous for his drug that cured my paralysis. It was a long haul back to full health again, with a (for me) terrible time working in the special unit, doing exercises with his specially designed gadgets to bring back the old power to my limbs.

I made the acquaintance of the grouchy old pathologist who had sat at Sir Russington's bench on those occasions when I went in and got ticked off, because without knowing it, I had interrupted some very special research. Of course, the old boy could have put the 'Keep Out' notice on the door outside, but the old chap would never allow that that was the case. I was at fault, by interrupting him, so of course, I got the rough edge of his tongue, which amused Jeff inordinately when I told him, that day on the shore, and he then realized why I had thought the old chap was Richard's uncle.

'I never thought I'd be able to keep up the deception,' Jeff told me one day, after I had retired from my exercises so limp with fatigue that I didn't care what he said or did.

He carried me to the lounging chair in his private office and sat with me cuddled in his arms, and he said, 'I never could believe it when I saw, each time, that you still didn't know who I was. And then it got out of hand, and I was in a shocking quandary in case you did find out, because by then, the further it went on, the worse it got and I knew you'd never forgive me!'

'I might have,' I allowed. 'But what I didn't forgive was seeing you driving off that day with Heather.'

'I was doing my best to throw you and Richard together,' he said indignantly, but as always, he stopped the argument to kiss me and when he kissed me, there was no room for thoughts about anything else.

'You know, of course, that this is all wrong, me kissing the patient?' he demanded one day.

'Well, we're engaged . . . aren't we?' I retorted.

'Of course not! I haven't asked you to marry me yet,' he said.

That was always a joke between us, but somehow today it didn't have the hallmark of a joke about it.

I studied his frowning face. He didn't look as young as he used to. My illness had taken more out of him than either of us realized. I suppose that since he was the only one who could cure me (if anyone could) the responsibility had been terrible. Unlike Richard, who had kept cheerful and in high fettle with the thought of what that uncle of his could do, my dear Jeff had died a thousand deaths, at the thought of what might go wrong, because up till then his serum had only been tried out on animals.

In my usual way, I tried putting myself in his place, and imagining myself as the pathologist, and my heart twisted in me at the thought of his life resting precariously in my hands. I understood all right, what he had gone through. But now it was all over. It was a matter of time before I could get about again normally: time and special exercises. I went swimming with him as it was, and we got maximum pleasure out of that. But why didn't he ask me to marry him?

I watched him as he talked, that day. He introduced a thousand topics. Anything to keep off that thorny subject. He discussed Heather chiefly, and how that young man who had given her the lift and got her into that pile-up on the motorway, had been so insistent with his courting that even Heather had given in.

'Heather's marrying her actor-manager this week,' Jeff told me with a grin, 'so you won't have to ask me who I took out in the car when you weren't with me last.'

'I don't question you like that!' I said indignantly.

'Yes, you do! Well, you need not, any more. She's quite satisfied with him. The whole glittering world of stage and screen is before her now, and he isn't hard up. And she wasn't marked at all in that accident. She was very lucky.'

'Jeff, how was it that Heather didn't pick up the same bug as I did?' It was a question that had always intrigued me. 'She was with me at the time!'

He scowled. 'But she didn't clean out the bird cage. She didn't get a chill afterwards which left complications, and she never got over-tired working, as you did,' he said shortly.

Frances, now married to Charlie Ross, had long ago given up nursing. Charlie, I heard, was now absolutely fit, after a long time getting about with a stick. He had gone back to medicine because he wanted to, but Frances would never have to worry about finance — her husband's family were quite rich. I was so glad for her. And Richard was happy in his bachelorhood, looking forward to pathology, like his famous uncle.

But his famous uncle and I were as far apart as ever except that when we were alone he cuddled me and kissed me with a kind of desperation that I didn't understand. People told me I was almost cured, almost ready to go home and still my dear Jeff (as I always called him) had said nothing.

One particular day, after the exercises were over, and we were together, I felt I must know the truth. I got the idea that in spite of what people said, I hadn't long to live. I traced the lines on his face and said, 'I wish we could go back in time to that day on the beach when you first picked me up, when I got my feet tangled with that mess of hawser.'

'So do I,' he said unexpectedly, and then, hastily, he amended it. 'No, I don't, though! I wouldn't live through these last few months again, not for anything! NO!' he said violently.

'Ah, yes, but if I could go back again, I wouldn't be silly and . . . well, I wouldn't let myself be pushed into an engagement to Richard, as I did. I would say — '

'What would you say?' he broke in, as if he really wanted to know.

I had broken off in embarrassment.

'Well, don't look at me like that!' I begged him.

'Like what?' he asked, frowning.

I traced the lines with a tentative forefinger. 'You're being the well-known Sir Russington and not my Jeff, and when you're being that, I can't say or do anything.'

'But I *am* he,' he reminded me gently. 'I am not your Jeff. He was a make-believe figure. You know that, Eileen. A chap with my servant's name, that you met when he was off duty, and just at that time I was taking a sort of holiday. I didn't even go away, I wanted to do some of my work sometimes. The serum I used eventually on you,' he finished in a low voice.

I was surprised. 'You mean if you hadn't taken that sort of break, I wouldn't have seen you? You'd have gone off somewhere for a holiday, right away somewhere?'

He nodded. 'I usually took the *Seamaid II* to the Bahamas or the Mediterranean.'

I was shaken. How by a hair's breadth I had met him at all!

He still had his arms round me, but with a sigh, he put me away from him and got up. 'It was Fate, I suppose,' he said heavily.

I knew what he meant. If he hadn't kept on plugging at that serum, I would have died, helplessly paralysed. But there were other things to bother me now.

'Why do you keep cuddling me? I mean, you don't love me, do you? That is, you're not in love with me, are you?' I forced myself to say, though the colour was spreading up my face, which was so hot I dare not look at him. Not for nothing was he the hospital's Big Shot, the chap who got respect from everyone.

He came back to me and stared down at me, and I didn't understand his expression. 'I love you more than life, Eileen,' he said, on such a low note I almost didn't hear it.

'Then why — ?' I burst out. And as

usual, my impetuous tongue led me to say things common sense would have prevented me from saying. 'Then why don't you say so and ask me to marry you? Why did you make me get engaged to Richard? Why, you even made it a condition that we went to Switzerland to live and work!'

'I shouldn't have been able to bear the sight of you around, as someone's else's wife,' he said.

That was all very well, but it didn't explain anything. 'You can't love me, to give me away to someone else like that! You just can't!' I cried.

He seemed to be forcing himself to keep standing there, a few yards from me, when he really wanted to gather me into his arms again. He looked so drawn and tired, but he said, levelly enough, 'I had heard what was being said between your grandmother and yourself, that day in her cottage, and when I realized that you and Richard had cared for each other all your lives, I had to do everything in my power to make that possible.'

'Even to taking Heather out for the evening, openly, so that everyone knew I'd lost you?' I choked.

'I went further than that, long before that,' he admitted. 'It was I who gave her that extremely expensive brooch.'

I had guessed it, but it was still hard to bear. 'No! *Why?*'

He shrugged. 'To take her thoughts off Richard, and leave him for you! It worked, too, for a time.'

'But did you honestly think then, from what you knew of me, that I was still in love with Richard?' I cried. 'You *couldn't* have wanted to marry me!'

'Yes, I did believe you loved Richard, and what sort of man would I be, to ask you to marry me, believing it was an established thing between you and my nephew? A thing your grandmother and his father hoped for and accepted? I couldn't push in and break it up!' He breathed hard. 'When people love all their lives, it's usually for keeps, though they may not realize it.'

'Not when someone like Richard makes it plain he's happy unmarried,' I retorted. 'And not when a person meets someone like . . . like my Jeff, who just blotted out everyone else! Well, you did! Didn't you even know that?' and my voice broke.

He looked as if I was tearing him apart by the things I was saying. But still he didn't move. 'There are other complications now, Eileen,' he said at last. 'I can't let you be married, my dearest, not after that illness! I don't know how you'll be! How you'll stand up to marriage. And there's the question of children.'

'You know I want a family,' I said quickly, thinking perhaps he didn't, because of his work, the sort of life he led. And then, the dawning knowledge of what lay in his face struck me. 'You mean I can't have children?' I whispered. 'Is that it?'

He didn't answer but just looked stricken.

'Well, then I will have to do without

them. Oh, but you'll want children,' I said, remembering the way I had seen him with other people's children on the shore; the way he played with them. He loved children! They worshipped him! He would be a wonderful father.

'All right,' I said, covering my mouth with my hands because my lips were trembling so much. 'All right, you'd better marry someone else who can give you a family, but go away from me, do you hear? Because I love you so much, it's killing me, to be with you every day, and to know I can't . . . you won't . . . ' and that finished me.

He gathered me into his arms at that. We were neither of us fit for much, for some time.

At last, he said, with difficulty, 'Very well, I'll take the risk. You want marriage. Perhaps it will be all right. But my darling, I don't *know*. Don't you see? You're the first, the first one I've cured. I don't know what sort of cure it is, what limitations there are, what side effects — what can be enjoyed and what can't. Oh, Eileen . . . '

'Oh, Jeff!' I said briskly, pushing him away to look at him. I wiped my face with the back of my hand, and biffed his shoulder playfully. 'Where's your courage?' I demanded. 'Where's your *common sense*? Who *knows* how long they've got to live? Some people come into this hospital and don't go out — young people from the road crashes and the factory explosions. What would they have had of life if they'd been so cautious that they'd been afraid to get married in case they stepped under a bus? If people thought like that, why then, nobody would ever get married or have children or anything! Let me *try*, Jeff . . . that's if you really love me, really want me.'

'Oh, I do,' he choked, his voice muffled because his face was buried in my neck.

'Then ask me to marry you in the proper way,' I commanded, suddenly so light-hearted, so happy, so . . . every-thing. 'I've got faith! I believe in you, I believe you've cured me. And I'm going to be happy and enjoy a marvellous life! Are you listening to me, Jeff, love?' and I tried to turn his face up to mine.

He still had one or two more obstacles to put in the way. 'I'm nearly twice your age, Eileen,' he pointed out.

'That didn't stop you from being the bane of my life, when I thought you were only the dogsbody,' I retorted. 'That didn't stop you from arousing absolute hero-worship in those fisher-men's eyes every time they mentioned the way you handled the *Seamaid II* in dirty weather, single-handed. It didn't stop you doing any of the things people admired you for — with style, superbly!' I reminded him.

'And I'm Richard's uncle,' he tried again. 'What about that?'

So I retorted, 'If you keep raising obstacles I shall begin to think you don't love me and don't want to marry me!'

He kissed me then, in such a way that made that last remark seem quite superfluous, and very silly. And for good measure he said, his face hidden, 'I'm as sick and silly with love for you as . . . well, as the other chaps used to get, over Heather!'

And while I succumbed to his kisses, that last remark of his washed over me with all its significance, and it was poetry, it was security, it was all I'd ever wanted. Jeff loved me with all his heart, and he was all mine, for ever.

We do hope that you have enjoyed reading this large print book.

Did you know that all of our titles are available for purchase?

We publish a wide range of high quality large print books including:
Romances, Mysteries, Classics
General Fiction
Non Fiction and Westerns

Special interest titles available in large print are:
The Little Oxford Dictionary
Music Book, Song Book
Hymn Book, Service Book

Also available from us courtesy of Oxford University Press:
Young Readers' Dictionary
(large print edition)
Young Readers' Thesaurus
(large print edition)

For further information or a free brochure, please contact us at:
Ulverscroft Large Print Books Ltd.,
The Green, Bradgate Road, Anstey,
Leicester, LE7 7FU, England.
Tel: (00 44) **0116 236 4325**
Fax: (00 44) **0116 234 0205**

Other titles in the
Linford Romance Library:

A LITTLE BIT OF CHRISTMAS MAGIC

Kirsty Ferry

As a wedding planner at Carrick Park Hotel, Ailsa McCormack is organising a Christmas Day wedding at the expense of her own holiday. Not that she minds. She's always been fascinated by the place and its past occupants; particularly the beautiful and tragic Ella Carrick, whose striking portrait still hangs at the top of the stairs. And then an encounter with a tall, handsome and strangely familiar man in the drawing room on Christmas Eve sets off a chain of events that transforms Ailsa's lonely Christmas into a magical occasion . . .

DOCTOR'S LEGACY

Phyllis Mallett

When Dr Helen Farley arrives in the Cornish fishing village of Tredporth as a locum, she feels instantly at home, and is fascinated by the large house standing on the cliffs. Owned by the ageing Edsel Ormond, her most important patient, the estate has two heirs: Howard and Fenton, Edsel's grandsons. But when Edsel informs Helen that he's decided to leave the property to Howard alone, on the condition that he first marries — and that the woman must be *her* — she realises her problems are only just beginning . . .

ROAD TO ROMANCE

Christine Lawson

A photography competition lands Penny Maxwell far from her job at the village bakery shop into the bright spotlight of fame. But she hasn't counted on the machinations of Robina Trent, who sees her likeness in the newspaper and realises they are virtual doubles. When Robina begins to make appearances in Penny's name, no one else is in on their secret. But little does Penny realise that loneliness and heartache will follow — for the man she loves, pianist Paul Hambledon, is stunned by the deep change in her . . .

ON THE MARRAM SHORE

June Davies

Catriona Dunbar is sent to stay with relatives on the Lancashire coast for the season. But between perpetually drunken Samuel Espley and his caddish son Julian, life in the grand house of Pelham is far from the happy holiday she had been anticipating. The only consolation is her growing friendship with the hired hand Morgan Chappel: a bond that seems poised to blossom into something more. Until Morgan is arrested — and Catriona must make a devil's bargain to save him . . .

NURSE CALEY OF CASUALTY

Quenna Tilbury

On Barbara Caley's first shift in Casualty, Damien Elridge, a film star, and his fiancée Margaret Knowles are brought in from a car accident. Damien has promised Margaret a part in a film, but an argument before the crash has put both that and their prospective marriage into doubt — and when Damien meets Barbara, he immediately expresses an interest in her. But Barbara is already in love with Adam Thorne, the Casualty Officer, who is also Margaret's ex-fiancé. Can the quartet find their way through the tangle to happiness?

THE DEFENDING HEART

Delia Foster

Judy Henderson finds herself in the wrong place at the wrong time on three fateful occasions. She witnesses her first employer fall out of her window, and her second employer she discovers dead at the foot of the stairs. Then there's the nurse she sees pushed off a train. Dr David Marland is the only person who believes Judy's fantastic tales — and how is her enigmatic boyfriend involved? Together, Judy and David must uncover the terrifying truth that links the deaths — before more are added to the list . . .